STORIES ON WOMEN

Stories on

WOMEN

PREMCHAND

Edited with an Introduction by
M. Asaduddin

Translated from Hindi and Urdu by
M. Asaduddin and others

PENGUIN

VIKING

An imprint of Penguin Random House

VIKING

USA | Canada | UK | Ireland | Australia
New Zealand | India | South Africa | China

Viking is part of the Penguin Random House group of companies
whose addresses can be found at global.penguinrandomhouse.com

Published by Penguin Random House India Pvt. Ltd
7th Floor, Infinity Tower C, DLF Cyber City,
Gurgaon 122 002, Haryana, India

Published in Viking by Penguin Random House India 2018

These stories were first published as *Premchand: The Collected
Short Stories Volumes 1-4* in Penguin Books 2017

Introduction copyright © M. Asaduddin 2018
The copyright for the English translations vests with the respective translators

ISBN 9780670091430

Typeset in Adobe Garamond Pro by Manipal Digital Systems, Manipal
Printed at Replika Press Pvt. Ltd, India

www.penguin.co.in

Contents

Introduction

Premchand is generally regarded as the greatest writer in Urdu and Hindi both in terms of his popularity and the range and depth of his corpus. His enduring appeal cuts across class, caste and social groups. He was not only a creative writer in Urdu and Hindi, but fashioned modern prose in both and influenced several generations of writers. The fact that his works were published in more than two dozen Hindi and Urdu journals simultaneously attest to his extraordinary reach to a wide audience that formed his readership. Many of his readers encountered modern Urdu and Hindi novels and short stories, and indeed any literary form, for the first time through his writings. Premchand's unique contribution to the formation of a readership—and, in turn, to shaping the taste of that readership—is yet to be assessed fully. Few or none of his contemporaries in Urdu–Hindi have remained as relevant today as he is in the contexts of the Woman Question (*Stree Vimarsh*), Dalit Discourse (*Dalit Vimarsh*), Gandhian Nationalism, Hindu–Muslim relations and the current debates about the idea of an inclusive India.

Born Dhanpat Rai (1880–1936) in Lamhi, a few miles from Banaras, Premchand's childhood was spent in the countryside. Called 'Nawab' at home, his early schooling was in Urdu and Persian, much in the Kayastha tradition of the time. He also attended the mission school where he studied English along with other subjects. His father was a postal clerk who moved from place to place. When Premchand was only seven his mother died and his father remarried. His relationship with his stepmother was never cordial. He was married at an early age against his wish to a girl who was totally incompatible and he refused to live with her. His second marriage, to a young widow with literary interests, Shivrani, proved to be a happy one. When he was seventeen his father suddenly died and the responsibility of running the family fell on him. He was forced to discontinue his studies and take up the job of a school teacher. However, after his graduation in 1904 he became a sub-deputy inspector of schools, a job which required substantial travel which did not agree with his frail health. In 1921, he gave up government service at the call of Gandhi during the Non-Cooperation movement.

Premchand began writing in 1905 and contributed articles on literary and other subjects in the Urdu journal *Zamana*. His first short stories were also published in this journal. In fact, Premchand began his career as a short story writer with the publication of *Soz-e-Watan* (Lament for the Motherland, 1908), written under his pen name, Nawab Rai. The collection drew the attention of the colonial government because of its alleged radical intent. He was summoned, when he was on an inspection tour, to explain his position. This is how Premchand describes the situation in his own words:

> . . . Those days I wrote under the name of Nawab Rai. I already had some information that the intelligence wing of the police was making inquiries to track down the author of the book. I could realize that they have found me out and I had been summoned to defend myself.
>
> The Saheb asked, 'Have you written this book?' I admitted that I had.
>
> The Saheb then asked me to explain the subject matter of each story, and finally burst out in anger, 'Your stories are full of sedition. Thank God that you are a servant of the British Empire. Had this happened during the Mughal rule both your hands would have been chopped off.'[1]

He was asked to burn all the copies of the book, and henceforth, get prior permission from the administration before sending any writing for publication. Petrified, he abided by the demands of the magistrate and submitted all available copies of the book to his office to be destroyed. Premchand realized that writing under the name Nawab Rai was no longer safe and sustainable, and to circumvent the iron hand of colonial censorship he had to assume a new pseudonym, which was Premchand. Thus, both Dhanpat Rai and Nawab Rai were

---

[1] 'Munshi Premchand ki Kahani Unki Zubani' in *Zamana* (Premchand Number), 1938. Reprinted by National Council for Promotion of Urdu Language, July 2002, p.54.

finally buried and Premchand was born, a name by which generations of readers would know him.

Themes

Caste

Premchand felt a deep affinity with the common man and his natural sympathy was towards the oppressed and deprived sections of society. No writer before him in Urdu or Hindi, and possibly other Indian literatures, had depicted the lives of the underdogs, the untouchables and the marginalized with such depth and empathy. Throughout his life 'Premchand did not let go of his unsentimental awareness of the grim realities of rural life, of life at the bottom of the economic scale' (Amrit Rai: 1982, ix). The oppressors and oppression came in many forms—they may have been priests or zamindars, lawyers or policemen or even doctors, all of whom held the society in their strangle-hold. Rituals pertaining to Hindu marriages and death were so exploitative and oppressive that these events were often robbed of their dignity and joy and spelt the ruin of families.

Premchand began his career by exposing the corruption of the Hindu priestly class in his novel *Asraar-e-Muavid* (Mysteries of the House of Worship, 1903–05), and then he continued the tirade in many of his stories. In the story 'Babaji's Feast' 'Babaji ka Bhog' he depicts the greed of the Brahmin baba who has no compunction in robbing a poor family of its meagre means, and in 'Funeral Feast' 'Mritak Bhoj' he showed how the predatory and parasitical Brahmins drive another Brahmin woman to destitution and her daughter to suicide. In a series of stories where the central character is Moteram, a Brahmin priest, Premchand exposes with rare courage the rapacity, the hollowness and hypocrisy of the Hindu priestly class, which earned him the ire and venom of a section of high-caste Hindus, even culminating in a law suit for defamation. But he remained undaunted and went on exposing many oppressive customs that were prevalent in society.

But his most trenchant critique was reserved for caste injustice whereby people at the lowest rung of the Hindu caste system were considered untouchables and were compelled to live a life of indignity and humiliation. The upper-caste Hindus treated them as worse than animals and this injustice was institutionalized through social sanction of the caste system. Stories such as 'The Well of the Thakur' 'Thakur ka Kuan', 'Salvation' 'Sadgati', 'Shroud' 'Kafan', 'Temple' 'Mandir', 'The Woman Who Sold Grass' 'Ghaaswali' and 'One and a Quarter Ser of Wheat' 'Sawa Ser Gehun' constitute a devastating indictment of the way the upper-caste Hindus have treated the Dalits for generations. The stories demonstrate that the Dalits were subjected to daily humiliation by members of the upper castes and this humiliation stemmed from the fact that Dalit inferiority had become embedded in the psyche of the members of the Hindu upper castes who had developed a vast repertoire of idioms, symbols and gestures of verbal and physical denigration of the Dalits over centuries. Grave injustice and inhuman treatment of the Dalits had become normalized, causing no revulsion against it in society. Despite criticism from some Dalit ideologues levelling some rather irresponsible charges against Premchand for depicting Dalits in a certain way, these stories—some of which have been rendered into films—have contributed significantly in raising awareness about the injustice perpetrated against the most vulnerable section of society.

Women

A considerable number of his stories deal with the plight of women. Premchand was deeply sensitive to the suffering of women in a patriarchal society where women had no agency and had to live their lives according to the whims and fancies of men on whom they had to depend—husbands, fathers, brothers or even close or distant male relatives. Women were expected to be docile, submissive and self-effacing, sacrificing their lives for the well-being of the family. Girls were treated as a curse to the family and their parents were subjected to all kinds of humiliations and indignities while arranging their marriage. Parents were sometimes compelled to marry off their nubile and very young daughters to old men just to unburden themselves of the responsibility and shame of being saddled with an unmarried daughter. The practices of *kanya vikray* (sale of a daughter in marriage), even *kanya vadh* (killing of a girl child) too were prevalent.

In his essays and editorials, Premchand made a strong plea for the abolition of the evil practices that made the life of women unbearable. He supported divorce in extreme circumstances, backed the wife's claim to half of the husband's property in case of divorce and inherit the property in case of the husband's death. He also wrote in favour of the Sarda Bill which aimed at raising the minimum age of marriage of girls. In a large number of stories, such as 'Tuliya' 'Devi',

'Sati', 'Goddess from Heaven' 'Swarg ki Devi', 'Return' 'Shanti', 'Godavari's Suicide' 'Saut', 'Thread of Love' 'Prem Sutra', 'Two Friends' 'Do Sakhiyaan', 'The Lunatic' 'Unmaad' and so on, he sheds light on the plight of women in an oppressive, patriarchal system. Through the immortal characters of old women like the Chachi in 'Holy Judges', the Old Aunt in the eponymous story and Bhungi in 'A Positive Change' 'Vidhwans', he shows how difficult life was for old women in a society that was known to respect its elderly members. The fate of widows, who were considered inauspicious and were expected to renounce all joys of life, was even worse, as shown in 'Compulsion' 'Nairashya Leela', 'The Condemned' 'Dhikkar' and 'A Widow with Sons' 'Betonwali Vidhva'.

The Village and the City

Premchand's love for the countryside is evident in his fictional and non-fictional writings. He has written several extremely evocative stories such as 'Panchayat', 'Do Bail', 'Idgah', 'Atma Ram', depicting the pristine village life of simplicity, honesty and quiet contentment. In fact, his fictional corpus, if read uncritically, would lend itself to an easy binary between country life and city life, one good and the other almost irredeemably evil. Yet, we have to recognize that he does not depict country life as an idyll shorn of all evils. There are stories such as 'A Positive Change' 'Vidhwans', 'A Home for an Orphan' 'Grihdaah' and 'The Road to Salvation' 'Mukti Marg' that de-romanticize and demystify village life and depict the author's awareness of the imperfections and blind spots in the supposed idyll. Thus, the apparent binary that seems to work in case of some novels and stories cannot be stretched beyond a point.

Animals

Premchand's deep interest in the simple life of peasants extended to his love for animals, particularly draught animals, treated most cruelly in India. Very few writers have depicted such an intimate bond between animals and human beings. Premchand depicts animals as endowed with emotions just as human beings are, responding to love and affection just as human beings do, and are fully deserving of human compassion. Often, the duplicity, cruelty and betrayal in the human world is contrasted with the unconditional love and loyalty displayed by animals towards their masters and those who care for them. It is a heart-wrenching moment, as shown in 'Money for Deliverance' 'Muktidhan' and 'Sacrifice' 'Qurbani' when a peasant has to part with his animals because of want and destitution. The deep compassion with which animal life has been depicted in 'Holy Judges' 'Panchayat' 'Reincarnation' 'Purva Sanskar' 'The Story of Two Bullocks' 'Do Bailon ki Katha' and 'The Roaming Monkey' 'Salilani Bandar' are treasures of world literature. Stories such as 'Turf War' 'Adhikar Chinta' and 'Defending One's Liberty' 'Swatt Raksha', written in a humorous and symbolic vein, show how a dog fiercely protects his turf and how a horse defeats all the machinations of human beings to make him work on a Sunday which is his day of rest, rightfully earned after working for six days of the week! In 'The Roaming Monkey', the author shows how a monkey earns money by showing tricks of different kinds and thus looks after the wife of his owner, nurtures her and brings her back from the brink of lunacy. In 'The Price of Milk' 'Doodh ki Qeemat' we have the spectacle of goats feeding a baby with milk from their own udders, thereby saving its life.

Premchand's Style

The atmosphere of dastaan and historical romances hangs heavy on Premchand's early stories. But he soon grew out of that phase and made his work more socially relevant by giving it the hard, gritty texture of realism. His art of storytelling became a vehicle for his socially engaged agenda of social reform and ameliorating the condition of the deprived and oppressed sections of society. However, that does not mean he was mainly concerned with the content and external circumstances of his characters and not with their inner worlds. Like all great writers, he took interest in unravelling the mental processes of his characters and the psychological motivations of their actions. As he says:

> My stories are usually based on some observations or personal experience. I try to introduce some dramatic elements in them. I do not write stories merely to describe an event. I try to express some philosophical/emotional reality through them. As long as I do not find any such basis I cannot put my pen to paper. When this is settled, I conceive characters. Sometimes, studying history brings some plots to mind. An event does not form a story, as long as it does not express a psychological view of reality.[2]

---

[2] 'Premchand ki Afsana Nigari', *Zamana*: Premchand Issue, February 1938; rpt. National Council for Promotion of Urdu (New Delhi, 2002), p. 173.

In the stories he has written one finds different modes and points of view, which he adopted by employing an array of narrative devices. An overwhelming number of his stories are written in the third person or omniscient narrative mode and a far lesser number in the first person. He makes extensive use of dialogue, using different registers of Urdu and Hindi in addition to dialects, colloquialisms, idioms and speech patterns specific to a caste, class or community. He also uses the technique of interior monologue and multiple points of view in quite a few stories. The salient point is that even though Premchand was mainly concerned with the content of his stories, to the extent of sometimes making them formulaic and predictable, he certainly did engage with the stylistic aspects too. And in this respect, he was influenced by both Indian—specifically Bengali—and foreign writers.

M. Asaduddin

Tulia

1

Tulia lacked the childlike brazenness that is typical of old age. Her hair had turned snow-white and her cheeks had developed wrinkles. She couldn't tell her age herself, but everybody's guess was that she was more than a hundred years old. She still covered her head with the *pallu* of her sari, her eyes downcast, as though she were a newly married daughter-in-law. She was from the tanner caste but without any greed for tasty food. There were many high-caste families in the village. Tulia went to every house. The entire village held her in esteem and the housewives had great regard for her. They invited her to their houses, oiled her hair and put sindoor on her hair parting. They wanted to feed her if any delicacies were prepared that day like halwa or kheer, but the old woman loved her self-respect more than the flavour of delicacies. She never ate the stuff. She had no one to call her own. Some of her people had left the village, some had died of the plague and malaria. The ruins left by them stood naked, as if in mourning. Only her shack stood there. She had reached that stage of her life when a human being becomes free from all shackles of religion and society. Now even the best in the society didn't discriminate against her on grounds of her caste. Everyone was ready to give her shelter in their houses. But the self-respecting woman didn't accept favours from anyone. She didn't want to stain the honour of her master whose face she had seen just once, one hundred years ago. Just once!

Tulia was engaged when she was only five. Her husband was a strong young man of eighteen years. After marrying her, he had gone to the East to earn his livelihood. He had thought it'd be ten to twelve years before this girl came of age. During this period, he could earn some wealth and then work his land with ease of mind. Tulia came of age, then she became old, but he never returned. For fifty years, he sent a letter every three months. The letter contained an envelope with the address to which the reply should be sent. The letter was accompanied by a money order of thirty rupees. In his letters, he described his helplessness and lamented his fate: *What can I do, Tulia? I long to return, build my house and live with you happily. But everything depends on fate, we've no control over it. I'll come only when God brings me. Please have patience. I'll see to it that you've no difficulties as long as I live. I've taken my vows as your husband, and will continue to keep them till my death. Who knows what will happen when I meet my end.*

All his letters conveyed the same sentiments with slight difference of phraseology. Of course, the letters that he wrote during his youth conveyed his pain of separation, but the more recent ones were full of despair. For Tulia all the letters were equally dear, they were quite close to her heart. She hadn't torn a single letter—no one had the heart to tear them. They had made a thick bundle. The papers had lost colour, the ink had faded, but for Tulia they were a living reality. All of them were tied in red ribbon and stored in a box. They epitomized for her the love for her husband, accumulated over long years. These letters brought her happiness. She would often get someone to read them and she shed tears over them. On that day she would put oil in her hair, get sindoor on her hair parting and wear a colourful sari. She would touch the feet of her elders and take their blessings. Her love for her husband would rekindle. For women in the village whose husbands lived far away, a letter wasn't something that they just read and threw away, it symbolized the life of their husbands, dearer than the body. This sentiment is devoid of physical cruelty or pollution and expresses yearnings of the soul and true love. For Tulia, the letters were a substitute for her husband. She hadn't seen him in any other form.

Women teased her, 'Aunty, do you have any memory of Uncle? You must've seen him.'

Tulia's face would light up for a moment amidst the wrinkles that criss-crossed it, her eyes would sparkle. She would say, 'Why shouldn't I have any memory of him? His shape is before my eyes even today. He had large eyes, blood red. His forehead was broad and his chest was wide. He had a robust body, the like of which is rare these days. His teeth were pearl-white, son. He was wearing a red kurta. When we got married, I told him, "I won't go to your house unless you get a lot of jewellery made for me." It was childishness, son; there was no question of shame or modesty then. Hearing this, he burst into a peal of laughter, placed me on his shoulders, and said, "I'll have a lot of jewellery made for you, Tulia; how much can you wear? I'm going faraway to earn a livelihood. I'll send you money from there; you can then get a lot of jewellery made. I'll even bring a case of jewels with me when I'll return from there." Son, I was sent in a palanquin to my in-laws' house; how on earth would my parents be capable of inviting my husband to our house along with the *baraatis*! It was only at his place that I was betrothed to him. Within a single day, he had impressed me so much that when he was leaving, I embraced him, cried, and said, "Take me along with you. I'll cook for you, prepare your bed and clean your dhoti." A couple of people his age were sitting there. Right before them, he smiled and said in my ears, "And won't you sleep with me?" That was it. I detached myself from him and stood at a distance. I then hurled a stone at him and said, "You better not abuse me, I'm telling you!"'

And through daily reminiscence and rosary, this life story had become a life mantra. Her face made quite a sight at such moments! It glowed! She would remove her veil, gesticulate, turn her face and smile as though there were no sorrows in her life. She would recount the sacred memories of her life and flash this light from the depth of her heart that saved her from the thorns of life for a hundred years. What a longing it was that couldn't be wiped out by the hard realities of life.

2

There was a time when Tulia was a young woman. She was beautiful and moths would hover around the candle of her beauty. When she narrated in her trembling voice with her tearful eyes the tales of their love and madness and surrender, the souls of these martyrs probably danced in heaven. What they didn't get when alive, Tulia was now giving them with both hands. She was a full-blooded woman. Wherever she went, young men pined for her. There was a Thakur whose name was Bansi Singh. He was a carefree and fun-loving young man whose songs reverberated far into the desolation of the night. He made rounds of Tulia's house a hundred times a day. He followed her like a shadow, on the bank of the pond, in the fields near the well, indeed wherever she went. Sometimes he took milk to her house, and sometimes buttermilk. He'd say, 'Tulia, I don't want anything from you. Just accept whatever gift I give you. Don't talk to me if you don't want to, don't look at my face if you don't feel like, but please don't turn down my gifts. I'll be happy if you accept them.' Tulia wasn't so innocent. She knew very well that he was simply biding for an opportunity. But one day, she somehow got into the trap—no, not really—she, in fact, took pity on his youth. One day, he brought her a basket of mangoes, freshly plucked from the orchard. Tulia had never eaten such freshly plucked mangoes. She took the basket from him. From then on, he began to gift her a basket of mangoes every other day. One day, when Tulia took the basket from him and was entering her house, Bansi quietly caught her hand and placed it on his chest. He fell at her feet and said, 'Tulia, if you don't take pity on me even now, then kill me today. Let me die in your hands. This is my only wish.'

Tulia flung the basket on the ground, disentangled her legs, moved one step back, and said with wrathful eyes, 'Enough, Thakur, go away from here, else either you won't live or I won't. Your mangoes can rot for all I care. Is my husband only living for my sake across the black sea miles away from here so that I should be false to him? He is a man

who earns his livelihood; couldn't he afford another wife? Is
there any dearth of women in the world? But he hasn't done
it for my sake, even being a man. He is no less sturdy than
you, even if he may not be as glamorous. Do you want to read
the letters that he sent to me? Wherever he is, he sends money
to me regularly, even though I don't ask him to. Is he doing
all this so that I entertain other men? As long as he'll consider
me as his own, Tulia will stay loyal to him, in mind as well as
in actions. When I was married to him, I was a wayward girl
of five years. What happiness could I have given him? But he
has stayed loyal to the bond. Being a man if he can be loyal,
how can I be disloyal to him being a woman?'

Tears were streaming down the Thakur's face and his
lips were fluttering. It looked as though he wanted to be
swallowed by the earth.

After a moment, he folded his hands and said, 'I've
committed a great crime, Tulia. I haven't known you well.
The proper punishment for this is that you kill me right at
this moment. A sinner like me can obtain salvation only in
this way.'

Tulia didn't take pity on him. She felt that this man was
still trying to hoodwink her. She said, annoyed, 'You should
die, if you want to. Are there no wells in the world? Can't you
find a sword or a dagger? Why should I bother to kill anyone?'

The Thakur looked at her with despairing eyes, 'So this
is your command?'

'Why should you wait for my command? Those wanting
to die don't wait for anyone's command.'

The Thakur went away. The following day people saw
his body floating in the river. They thought that he must
have gone for a bath in the river early in the morning and

had drowned. People talked about him for months, but Tulia didn't utter a word. She stopped going in that direction.

As soon as Bansi Singh died, his younger brother took over his property and began to torment the widow and son. Her *devar* found fault with her and his wife made caustic comments. Eventually, the hapless widow couldn't bear it any more and left the house for good. The village was deep in sleep. Tulia had taken her dinner and was going to feed the cow some roti, holding the lantern in her hand. He saw the widow of the Thakur in the light of the lantern, advancing slowly. She was crying and wiping her tears with her sari. She was holding her three-year-old son with her arms.

Tulia asked her, 'Where are you going, thakurain, at this late hour? Listen, what is the matter? Oh dear, you're crying.'

The thakurain was going away from her house, but she herself didn't know where. With stoic eyes, she looked once at Tulia and moved forward without saying anything. How could she reply? Her throat was already filled with tears and she didn't know why they were brimming over, all the more at this instant.

Tulia came before her and said, 'Unless you tell me, I won't allow you to go even a step further.'

The thakurain stopped, filled her tearful eyes with fury, and said, 'Why do you ask? It's none of your business.'

'None of my business? Don't we live in the same village? If the villagers won't help each other out in their moments of sorrow and distress, then who'll do so?'

'Whoever supports anyone these days in this world, Tulia? Whom should I expect from, when my own in-laws didn't support me and became bloodthirsty as soon as your bhaiya passed away? Isn't everything known to you regarding the situation of our house? There is no place for me there. The very devar and *devarani* for whom I did everything, have now become my enemies. They just want us to be satisfied with a mere roti and want us to lie in a corner like orphans. I'm not a concubine and I didn't elope either. I'm a married woman; I was betrothed amidst people belonging to ten different villages. I won't relinquish even the least bit of my property. They may not give me anything now as I'm helpless. I may lose all my self-respect, but I'll ruin them and will certainly take my half.'

'Your bhaiya,'—these two words felt so dear to Tulia that she hugged the thakurain, held her hands, and said, 'In that case, sister, come and stay in my house. Others may support you or not, but Tulia will certainly support you till her death. My house is not suitable for your stay, but at least there is peace in it, if nothing else. And I'm still your sister, no matter how lowly I may be.'

The thakurain fixed her astonished gaze at Tulia's face. 'It shouldn't happen that my devar should become your enemy too, behind my back.'

'I'm not scared of my enemies and I don't live alone in this hamlet either.'

'But I don't want you to get into trouble because of me.'

'Who is going to tell them anyway, and who'll ever find out that you're inside my house?'

The thakurain found some solace. She hesitantly came inside with Tulia. Her heart was heavy. Someone who was the landlady of a stately concrete mansion was lying in this shack today.

There was only one cot in the house; the thakurain would sleep on it with her child. Tulia slept on the floor. There was only one blanket—the thakurain covered herself with it while Tulia would spend her nights by covering herself with a sackcloth.

She would only think about how to look after her guests properly. She would wash the thakurain's utensils, wash her clothes and feed her baby with utmost sincerity. It was as though she was worshipping a deity. The thakurain couldn't forget her status even though she had fallen on bad days. She was vain, brainless, and loved luxury. She lived there as though it was her own house and treated Tulia with such aggression as though she was her slave. But Tulia was maintaining her relationship with the wife of her unfortunate lover. She didn't mind her bad behaviour. There was never a frown on her face.

One day, the thakurain said, 'Tulia, please look after the child. I'll go somewhere for a couple of days. The way it is going, I'll sponge on you throughout my life for my daily bread, but how will my heart's fire be cooled? That shameless person doesn't even care where his brother's wife has gone. He must be happy in the thought that the only obstacle standing in his way has been removed. The moment he gets to know that I've not gone to my parents' house but stayed elsewhere, he'll promptly try to spread slander against me, and then the entire society will be on his side. I should think of a way out of this.

Tulia asked, 'Where do you want to go, sister? Do you mind if I accompany you? Where will you go alone?'

'I'll look for a way to beat him at his own game .'

Tulia couldn't understand the meaning of this. She stared at her face.

The thakurain asked brazenly, 'You couldn't even understand such a simple thing! So, you want me to spell it out clearly? What weapon does a widow have for her defence other than her beauty? Now, I'll only take recourse to this weapon. Do you even know what the price of this beauty shall be? It'll be that wolf's head! My charm will only work on whosoever may be the lord of this district's subdivision. And what man has ever been able to escape a maiden's charm even though he might be an ascetic? My dharma may get compromised for all I care. I can't bear to watch myself plucking leaves from various forests while that rogue twists his whiskers and rules here.'

Tulia realized how deep the wound was in this vain woman's heart. She was not only living her life on the edge, but was also sacrificing her dharma to placate her anguish. That very dharma that was dearer to her than her own life. The supplicating image of Bansi Singh appeared before her eyes. He was strong and could've easily used force against Tulia. And who would've saved her on that desolate night? But her reprimanding virtue captivated Bansi Singh in such a way as a deadly, black cobra gets intoxicated by listening to the melodious tune of a fiddle. The honour of that very hero's family was at stake today. Will Tulia allow this honour to be tainted and do nothing? No, it can't be! If Bansi Singh could privilege her virtue above his own life, then she too would preserve the thakurain's honour with her dharma.

She consoled the thakurain and said, 'Sister, don't go anywhere now. First let me test my strength. Who'll mock at me even if I lose my reputation? The honour of an entire family depends on your personal honour.'

The thakurain looked her with a smiling face. She said, 'What do you know about this art, Tulia?'

'What art?'

'Oh, the very skill of duping men.'

'Why, am I not a woman or what?'

'But you don't know about men's character, do you?'

'Oh, both of us have learnt about it from our mothers' wombs.'

'But tell me, what is it that you plan to do?'

'Oh, the very same that you were planning to. You wanted to work your charm on the ruler of this district's subdivision while I'll cast my spell on your devar.'

'He's very shrewd, Tulia.'

'That's what I want to see.'

3

Tulia spent the rest of the night thinking about the scheme and its execution. Like a skilled army commander, she had prepared a strategy that was similar to that of attack and carnage. She was convinced of victory. The rival was unsuspecting; he didn't even have the slightest idea about this attack.

Bansi Singh's younger brother Girdhar was haughtily coming this way with a thick club, six-feet long, on his shoulders when Tulia called out to him, 'Thakur, please pick this bundle of grass and put it on my head. I can't do it.'

It was noon. The labourers had returned from their fields. Whirlwinds had started blowing. Tulia stood under a tree with the bundle of grass. Her head was sweating profusely.

The Thakur looked at her in surprise. At that very instant, Tulia's sari slipped away and her red blouse flashed before his eyes. She quickly arranged her sari. But the flower braids in her hair in haste dazzled his eyes like lightning. Girdhar's mind became restless. His eyes showed mild intoxication and his face turned crimson while a faint smile played on his lips. Every vein of his body became taut.

He had seen Tulia a thousand times with thirsty, lusty eyes. But Tulia, lost in the vanity of her beauty and chastity, didn't look at him, ever. Her gestures showed such rudeness and cruelty that the Thakur would feel dispirited and his urges vanished. What impact could his net and food have on a bird flying freely in the sky? But today that bird had come on its own and was sitting on the nearby branch, and it seemed as though she was hungry too. Then why shouldn't he cast his net and throw his food?

He said in an intoxicated tone, 'I'll take the bundle to your home, you needn't carry it on your head.'

'And if someone sees it, what'll he think of you?'

'I don't care if the dogs bark.'

'But I do.'

The Thakur didn't listen to her. He heaved the bundle on his head. He was marching ahead as though he had got the wealth of the world.

4

A month passed by. Tulia had cast her spell on the Thakur and now she was playing with him as though he was a fish. Sometimes she would loosen the hook, while tightening it on other occasions. The Thakur had set out for hunting, but was himself trapped in the net.

Despite sacrificing his faith and his status, he couldn't receive the Goddess's blessings. Tulia was still at the same distance that she was at before.

One day, he said to Tulia, 'For how long will you tantalize me like this, Tulia? Come, let's elope somewhere.'

Tulia further tightened the noose and replied, 'Yes, that's what I thought. I won't be of any worth if you'll turn your face away from me. I'll lose both the worlds.'

The Thakur said with a complaining voice, 'Don't you believe me even now?'

'Bees fly away after collecting the flower's nectar.'

'And don't the moths burn and get reduced to ashes?'

'How should I trust you?'

'Have I ever disobeyed you?'

'You must be thinking that you'll be able to snare Tulia with a colourful sari and a couple of trinkets. I'm not that naive.'

Tulia had figured out the inner motives of the Thakur. He kept staring at her face in wonderment.

Tulia said again, 'A man always arranges for a dwelling place before leaving his house.'

The Thakur said happily, 'Come and be the mistress of my house. I've told you countless times.'

Tulia looked from the corner of her eyes and said, 'Today I'll live like the mistress, and tomorrow I'll not have the status of even a concubine, that's what you mean?'

'Do as you please. I'm your slave.'

'You give me your word of honour?'

'Indeed. Not once, but a thousand times.'

'Then you won't leave me?'

'Only an impotent person reneges on his word of honour.'

'Well, then make over half of your property in my name.'

The Thakur was ready to give her a cottage, a couple of bighas of land and some jewellery and clothes, but he didn't have the heart to make over half of his property in her name. Tomorrow, if she is displeased with him for any reason, then he'd have to wash his hands off the property. Who could rely on such a woman? He couldn't have imagined that Tulia would subject his love to such a severe test. He was furious. *This daughter of a tanner considers herself an apsara! My love for her was simply an infatuation for her beauty. It's not the kind of love for which one can sacrifice one's own self and everything else.*

He frowned and said, 'I knew that you were in love with my property, not me.'

Tulia wriggled herself out and replied, 'Didn't I know that you were in love with my beauty and youth, not with me?'

'You think love is bought and sold in the market?'

'Yes, I do. For you, love is a game for a couple of days. For me, it's the question of my life. When I'm giving you whatever I have, I want to extract its price. If you'd really loved me, you would have made over your entire property in my name. Will I carry the property with me? But I could see your real intentions. In a way, this is good. God forbid, a time comes when you've to stretch your hands before me— good days are never permanent for anyone; if ever such a time comes and you come to me, I'll show you how large a woman's heart is.'

Tulia left the place, annoyed. But she was not in despair, neither had she lost her heart. Whatever happened was part of her well-thought-out plan. She had no doubt about what was going to happen.

5

The Thakur had saved his property but at too great a cost. He lost the peace of his heart. It was as though nothing was left in his life. His property lay before his eyes while Tulia resided in his heart. Every day, she had appeared before him and had hurled shafts at his heart with her looks. She had been a concrete reality then. But the Tulia who was sitting in his heart now was a dream that was even more intoxicating and poignant than the truth.

Sometimes Tulia appeared like the flash of a dream and would vanish like the dream itself. Girdhar always looked out for an opportunity to share the anguish of his heart with her. But Tulia avoided even his shadow. Girdhar could now realize that she was more important than his property. He now felt angry at his stinginess. *What did it matter if the property was in her name or his? It was such a trivial matter. Tulia wanted this to be done so that in case I betrayed her, she wouldn't be helpless. Without her, I'm a worthless slave, so how can I be disloyal to her? I yearn for a glance, a word from her. How can I betray her? If I could see her alone, I would've said to her, 'Tulia, whatever I have is yours. I'll write whatever documents you want me to write. I'm ashamed of my fault. The natural weakness that a human being has for property made me say the words I said to you. This customary greed for money is standing between you and me. But now, I've realized that whatever gives joy in life is the most valuable object. If poverty and renunciation bring happiness, they should be the most coveted objects for which a man can sacrifice his land and property. Even today, there are such worthy sons of the soil who have renounced the world and its comforts, and have made jungles their abode. I couldn't understand such a simple thing. I was really unfortunate!'*

6

One day, Tulia sent a message to the Thakur: 'I'm sick. Come and visit me. Who knows whether I will survive or not?'

The Thakur hadn't seen Tulia for many days. Many a time, he would hover around her doorstep but he hadn't seen her. However, now that he had received the message, it was as if he had fallen down a mountainside. It must have been ten in the night. He didn't even listen to the whole thing and ran towards her house. His heart pounded and his head spun. *Tulia is sick! Oh God, what'll happen! Why don't you make me sick? I'm ready to die in her place.* The trees on both the sides loomed menacingly and seemed to chase him like two messengers of death. A voice issued intermittently from his throat—steeped in desire and pain. *Tulia is sick.*

His Tulia had sent for him. She had called for this thankless, vile and wretched assassin, saying, 'Come and visit me. Who knows whether I will survive or not?' *If you won't survive, Tulia, then even I won't live long. Alas! I won't. I'll die beating my head on the wall. Our pyres will be prepared together then and our funeral rites will be carried out simultaneously.*

He further hastened his steps. *Today, he'll lay everything that belongs to him at Tulia's feet. Tulia considers him unfaithful. Today, he'll show her how to keep the faith. If he wasn't faithful while living, he'll be so after his death. Whatever he wasn't able to do in this short span of his life, he'll do it for countless epochs. His love will become a legend and will be known in every house.*

A doubt crossed his mind. '*Will you be able to renounce the illusion of life?*' He beat his chest forcefully and shouted, 'For whom is this illusion of life? Moreover, my life is the very same—that of the one who is sick. Let me see, how death takes away life, leaving the body behind.'

He entered Tulia's house with his heart pounding and his legs shaking. Tulia was lying listlessly on her cot, wrapped in a sheet. In the dim light of the lantern, it seemed as if her pallid face was resting in the lap of death.

He put his head at her feet and said with a voice suppressed by tears, 'Tulia, this wretched one is lying at your feet. Won't you open your eyes?'

Tulia opened her eyes, cast a pitiful glance at him, and said, groaning, 'You're Girdhar Singh, aren't you? Have you come? Now, I'll die in peace. My heart was impatient to see you if only for the last time . Forgive me for what I ever said and never cry for me. What is this corporeal frame worth, Girdhar? Eventually, it'll merge with the earth. But I'll never leave your side. Like a shadow, I'll be with you forever. You won't be able to see or hear me, but Tulia will always remain with you. Girdhar, don't blame yourself because of me! Don't even mention my name before anyone. Yes, do sprinkle water on my pyre at least once. This will mitigate the fire burning in my heart.'

Girdhar started crying bitterly. Had there been a dagger in his hand, he would've pierced his heart at that very instant and died before her while writhing in pain.

Tulia took a deep breath and said again, 'I won't survive, Girdhar. Will you agree if I make a request?'

Girdhar beat his chest and said, 'My dead body will be carried out with yours, Tulia. What'll I do living now? And if at all I should live, how should I do so? You are my life, Tulia.'

He felt as though Tulia smiled.

'Oh, no, no. Don't be so stupid. You have a family and kids; look after them. If you truly love me, then don't do any such thing that may reveal this love, even slightly. Don't malign Tulia's name after her death.'

Girdhar cried and said, 'As you wish.'

'I just have a request for you.'

'I'll only live now to carry out your orders. This will be the sole mission of my life.'

'My only request is that you treat your *bhabhi* with the same respect and honour that she was accorded before Bansi Singh's death. Give her the share of the property that belongs to her—that is, half the property.'

'But she has been at her parents' house for the last three months and had said that she won't return ever.'

'Girdhar, you did wrong, very wrong. Now, I can understand why I would have nightmares. If you want me to recover, then have the documents read and signed as quickly as possible and leave it at my place. This stark dishonesty of yours has proved fatal for me. Now I know why Bansi Singh would repeatedly give me these dreams. I have no other disease. It's only Bansi Singh who is troubling me. That's it, go now. You won't find me alive if you delay. Bansi Singh is punishing me for your unjust deeds.'

Girdhar said in an undertone, 'But how can the documents be read and signed at night, Tulia? Where will I find the stamp paper? Who'll write out the documents? Where are the witnesses?'

'Girdhar, my life will be saved even if you'll get the documents read and signed by tomorrow evening. Bansi Singh is after me. He's the one who's been troubling me because he knows that you love me. I'm dying only because of your love. You won't find Tulia alive if you delay.'

'I'll go for now, Tulia. Your command is the topmost in my mind. You wouldn't have been reduced to this condition if you'd told me about this earlier. But it shouldn't happen that I may not be able to see you and my heart's longing will remain unfulfilled.'

'Oh no, no. Have faith. I won't die till tomorrow evening.'

Girdhar set out from there right at that moment and covered a distance of twenty-five miles—all during the night. He reached the town at daybreak, consulted the lawyers and made over half of the property in the name of his brother's wife. He got the property registered on stamp paper and before the evening lights were lit, he returned and stood before Tulia, trembling between hope and despair. He looked harassed and totally exhausted. It seemed as though he hadn't taken any food or water throughout the day. It was ten in the night. In those days, there were neither railways nor lorries. He had to trudge through fifteen *kos* of distance. He was so exhausted that every step felt like crossing a mountain. But he was afraid that if he did the slightest delay, then there would be a disaster.

Tulia asked happily, 'Have you returned, Girdhar? Is the job done?'

Girdhar placed the papers before her and said, 'Yes, Tula, I've done the job. But now even after all this if you don't get around, then I'll also die with you. I don't care if people make fun of me or they weep. I swear on you that I haven't taken even a drop of water.'

Tulia sat up and placed the paper near her headrest. She said, 'Now I'm much better. By morning, I'll be perfectly all right. I'll not forget your good act till I die. But a few moments ago, I had dozed off for a while and I dreamt that Bansi Singh was standing near my bed and telling me, "Tulia, you are a married woman. Your husband is sitting a thousand kos away from you but taking your name constantly. If he wanted, he could've married again. But he's waiting for you, and will do so for ever. If you betray him, then I'll become your enemy and rest only after taking your life. If you want your own good, then stay on the right path. I'll spell your ruin the day you betray him."

'Saying this, he glared at me with bloodshot eyes and left.' Girdhar looked at Tulia's face on which he could see a spiritual glow. It seemed as though a veil was lifted from his eyes and he could realize the intent of the entire plan. He touched Tulia's feet with the highest regard and kissed them. 'I can understand now, Tulia, that you are a goddess.'

Translated from the Hindi by Shailendra Kumar Singh

Sati

1

Mulia's husband, Kallu, comes nowhere close to her in good looks. Then why is it that Mulia is happy and satisfied but Kallu anxious and doubtful?

Mulia has a cowrie shell that nobody would care about. But Kallu has a gem that could have hundreds of buyers. He is especially cautious of his cousin Raja. He is handsome, a playboy, a glib talker who knows how to charm women. So Kallu does not allow Mulia to go out of the house. He cannot tolerate anybody eyeing her. He now works hard day in and day out to provide Mulia the comforts she deserves. He wonders what merit he might have gained in his previous birth to have the good fortune of a wife like her in this birth. He is willing to sacrifice himself for her. He gets distraught if Mulia has so much as a headache. Mulia too feels same for him. She yearns for him like a fish caught in a net until he comes back from work. There are so many young men in the village who try to flirt with her. But she considers her ugly Kallu far better than any of them.

One day Raja said, 'Bhabhi, my brother is not worthy of you.'

Mulia said, 'He was destined to be my husband, so how could I have found you?'

When he heard this, Raja thought that he had finally got the opportunity to impress Mulia. He said, 'Destiny faltered there.'

Mulia smiled and said, 'Well! If it did, then surely it will rectify its mistake.'

Raja was speechless.

2

Kallu brought a cotton sari for Mulia on the festival of Teej. He wanted to buy a nice sari for her, but did not have enough money for it, and the shopkeeper refused to give it on credit. Raja too wanted to test his fate. He brought a beautiful *chundari* for Mulia.

Mulia said, 'I have already got a sari.'

Raja said, 'I have seen it. That is why I got this for you. That sari is not worth your beauty. Bhaiya gets economical in such matters. He just buys the cheapest stuff available.'

Mulia subtly mocked him, 'Why don't you make him understand this?'

But Raja felt flattered. Drunk on arrogance, he replied, 'An old parrot cannot be made to learn.'

'I like my cotton sari.'

'Wear this chundari once, it will look wonderful on you.'

'If one is happy wearing coarse cotton, why would a beautiful chundari attract her? Had your bhaiya liked the chundari, he would have got one for me himself.'

'Do not show this to him.'

Mulia was amazed. 'Should I take it without even asking him?'

'Why do you need to ask? Wear it in his absence, when he goes out to work. I could see you then.'

Mulia laughed aloud and said, 'That is never going to happen, Devarji. He will get very angry if he sees it. You take it away.'

Raja pleaded with her, 'If you do not accept this, I will poison myself.'

Mulia put the sari in the alcove and said, 'All right, happy now?'

Raja held her by her finger and said, 'Bhaiya is not here now, wear it!'

Mulia went inside and wore the chundari. She looked as beautiful and radiant as a flower.

Raja held out his hands to her. 'I feel like running away with you.'

Mulia teased him saying, 'You know what will happen to your brother after that?' She shut the door on Raja's face. He felt as if somebody had snatched the plate from his hands right after serving the choicest delicacies.

3

Mulia wanted to show the chundari to Kallu but could not muster the courage to do it. She was afraid of his reaction. Why did she take the chundari? She was angry with herself. However, she justified her decision immediately—Raja would feel bad if she didn't. She had worn the chundari for only a moment. It was not an issue, it only made Raja feel good.

Something was gnawing at her heart. Why *did* she take the chundari? Was she cheating on Kallu? She was upset by the very thought of it. She tried to calm herself—this could not be cheating. She had not said anything to Raja. There was nothing wrong with laughing with someone if it made him happy. She had not crossed her limits.

Kallu asked her later in the day, 'What did Raju come for today?'

Mulia shivered with fear. She gave an excuse for Raju's presence—he had come to ask for tobacco.

Kallu knitted his brows and said, 'Don't let him enter the house. He is not a good man.'

'I told him there was no tobacco at home. So he went away.'

Kallu said heatedly this time, 'Why are you lying? He did not come for tobacco.'

'What else then?'

'Whatever it was, it was not for tobacco. He knows I do not have tobacco at home. In fact, I went to his house to ask for it.'

Mulia went pale with fear. The colour drained from her cheeks. She lowered her head and said, 'How would I have known his intentions?'

It was Teej today and all worshippers were to remain awake through the night. Mulia too was preparing for the puja, but not very enthusiastically. She went about it mechanically.

She was anxious, as if her face had been blackened. She had fallen in the eyes of Kallu. Her life had no meaning now.

It was anchorless. She thought—*Why did God give me such beauty? Had I been ugly, Raja would never have approached me. I would not have seen this day. Had I been unattractive and dark-complexioned, I would have been happier and at ease. My heart would not have been so restless. Those who want to encash their beauty flourish from it. Here, my beauty has destroyed everything.*

She fell asleep thinking these thoughts. She dreamt that Kallu had died and Raja was forcibly entering the house for her. An old woman had come from somewhere and was asking Mulia—'Why did you kill Kallu?' Mulia was saying while crying—'Mother, I have not killed him.' The old woman said—'Yes! You did not kill him with a knife and dagger. But you were not loyal to your husband and so he died.'

Mulia opened her eyes suddenly, waking up from the dream. Kallu was asleep in the courtyard. She started crying and ran to him. Apprehensive, Kallu asked her, 'Mula! Why are you crying? Are you afraid? Don't worry, I am awake.'

Mulia replied, 'I have committed a crime. Please forgive me.'

Kallu sat up and said, 'What is it? Why are you crying?'

'Raja had not come to ask for tobacco. I was lying.'

Kallu laughed, 'I knew it.'

'He had brought a chundari for me.'

'So you gave it back to him?'

Mulia shivered as she said, 'I took it. He threatened to poison himself if I did not take it.'

Kallu fell like a lifeless being on to the bed. He said, 'This beauty is beyond me. God has made me ugly, so how can I become attractive?'

Even if Kallu had thrown Mulia into a cauldron, she would not have suffered as much pain as she did now.

4

Kallu was very dejected after the incident. No enthusiasm and happiness remained in his life. He forgot how to laugh and talk. He had misunderstood Mulia and felt that she had cheated on him. Mulia's admission had deeply stung his heart. Now, his home was just another place to eat and sleep, and Mulia merely a machine to serve food. His sources of pleasure were limited to his frequent visits to a tavern and drugs.

Mulia was deeply frustrated seeing Kallu in such a state. She wanted to erase the feeling of distrust from his heart, and so she served him with all the care and love she had to offer. She tried her best to keep him happy, but it bore no fruit. The more she tried to pacify him, the more anxious he got, like a fish caught on a hook.

Fortunately, the British officer under whom Raja worked as a cook was transferred and Raja went away with him. Otherwise, chances of one killing the other were high.

A year passed like this.

One day, Kallu returned home with a fever. Next day, there were spots all over his body. Mulia thought it was measles, so she started praying to the goddess. However, the spots turned into boils after four or five days. It was found later that he was suffering from syphilis.

The disease was the result of Kallu's unhealthy lifestyle and sexual escapades.

His condition worsened as the boils filled up with pus, which reeked. Mulia treated Kallu with what she could afford in the village but his condition deteriorated with each passing day. She tried to compensate for the absence of medicine with her immense love and selfless service to Kallu. She had to work harder now to run the house as well.

Kallu was reaping the fruits of his sins. Mulia effaced herself completely while she looked after him. She had just one source of satisfaction, which was that Kallu's misunderstanding was gradually disappearing because of all her effort. He regained his trust in Mulia, that she was still his—*his* wife. If he got well now, he would hide her in his heart and worship her.

One morning, when Mulia was helping Kallu wash his face and giving him his medicine while fanning him, he said to her with tearful eyes, 'Mulia! I must have done some good work in my previous birth to have got a wife like you. I would not exchange you for the world's biggest empire.'

Mulia covered his mouth with her hands and said that she would cry if he said such things to her. 'It's my good luck that I have got a husband like you.' She put her arms around his neck and hugged him.

She said, 'God has punished me for my sins.'

Kallu asked her curiously, 'Tell me the truth, Mula. What happened between you and Raja?

Mulia was shocked. 'There was nothing between the two of us. Let God punish me if there was something between us. He had given me a chundari. I took it from him and burnt it. I have not spoken to him since then.'

Kallu sighed in relief. 'I misunderstood you. I doubted your fidelity, Mulia. I had lost my senses. I blamed you and indulged in sinful acts. I am paying for my sins now.'

He started crying and narrated his misdeeds to Mulia as she listened. She too was crying. She would have poisoned herself had she not been worried about her husband.

5

After some months, when Raja returned home on leave, he learnt about Kallu's deadly disease. He felt very happy and started visiting his house on the pretext of tending to Kallu.

Kallu turned his face whenever he saw Raja. But this did not deter Raja from visiting three or four times a day.

One day Raja stood at the door of the kitchen and asked Mulia, 'Bhabhi! Won't you still have mercy on me? You are so indifferent. You kept running away from me while I was yearning for you. Bhaiya will not get well now. His condition has become critical. Why are you ruining your life with him? Your flower-like body is all dried up. Come with me; let us relish the pleasures of life. This youth will not be around forever. See, I have brought these earrings for you. Wear them once for my sake.'

Mulia did not even look at them. Keeping her eyes on the stove, she said, 'Lala, I will touch your feet, please leave me alone. Don't do this to me. You are the one who brought this tragedy upon us. You are my enemy. Are you not ashamed to say your bhaiya is not worth anything now? I like him more than before now. Had I not been around, he would have married again. Today, he is dependent on me. If I betray him in this hour of need, I will be the greatest sinner.'

Raja laughed, 'You speak like one who, after he spills his curry, says he always preferred it like that.'

Mulia lifted her head and told him firmly, her eyes bright now, 'What do you say, Lala? You are nothing in comparison to my husband, not even the dust of his feet. A man does not become handsome just by wearing bright clothes and bearing good looks. I do not consider any other man as my husband's equal.'

Kallu called to her. 'Mula! Give me some water.' Mulia ran to him with water. The earrings lay in the courtyard, rejected.

Raja quickly picked them up and left the house in anger.

6

Kallu's disease worsened. Had he received proper treatment, he would have recovered, but what could Mulia have done on her own? Poverty and disease are not the best companions.

The final call for Kallu came at last. When Mulia came to attend to Kallu after her housework, she saw him taking laboured breaths. She trembled with fear and asked, 'How are you feeling?'

Kallu looked at her tearfully, folded his hands and lowered his head.

He bade farewell to the world. Mulia rested her head on his chest and wept bitterly. She was deeply hurt and words from her heart trickled like drops of blood—*Could you not see us together even this way, God! And people call you just and kind! Did you bring us into this world to toy with our lives? Is it a game for you? You were not so callous! Oh God!*

She called out to her Kallu, 'You have left me alone, who will call me Mula now? For whom shall I pull out water from the well? For whom will I make food? Whom will I feed and fan now? You have taken away my happiness, my only pleasure. Why not take me with you!'

The entire village gathered there. Everyone tried to pacify her but Mulia could not regain her calm. She was broken. 'All this happened because of me.' She could not forget her sorrow. Had God given her the strength, her husband, the centre of her life, would not have left her like this.

Preparations were made for the last rites.

7

Six months have passed since Kallu died. Mulia earns her own living now, eats and stays at home. She does not get any respite from the day's hard work. But yes, she often cries during lonely nights.

Meanwhile, Raja's wife had also passed away. He started roaming around the village like a loafer just days after her death. Earlier, he was at least fearful of the domestic scuffle. Now, there was no one to stop him. This time when he returned on leave, he went straight to Mulia's house and said, 'Bhabhi, will you not fulfil my desire now or is there still something left to be done? Bhaiya is no more. Even my wife has died. I have forgotten her. How long will you bemoan his absence?'

Mulia looked at him with hatred and said, 'Your bhaiya is no more but nothing has changed for me. His memories are still with me. His love and his face are still alive in my heart. His voice still rings in my ears. He is as alive for me now as he was earlier. He might have died for you but I see him sitting in front of me just as before. Earlier, we were still different bodies. Now, he has entered my soul and come closer to me than ever before. We have become one.'

She said, 'No one bothers about food in a fully stocked home; its importance is only realized when the house is empty. The rich do not care for the wads of money lying in their treasury but the poor worship every single penny they have. A poor man holds on to every cowrie for fear of losing it. God has not given you a heart, you see! So you do not know the importance of a spouse's company. It has not been more than six months since your wife passed away and here you are, a loose bull. Had you died instead of her, would she too have gone to seek solace in someone else's arms? I know for sure, had I died, my husband would have cried for me throughout his life. Wives die for such husbands and become satis. People like you can only lick from half-eaten plates. It is your fate. Lick it! But beware, don't you dare step into my house after this day, otherwise you will lose your life for sure! Just get out!'

Her face was so radiant and her words so cutting that Raja did not dare speak a word in response. He stepped out of the house quietly.

Translated from the Hindi by Bharti Arora

The Goddess from Heaven

1

It's all about destiny! Marriages are made in heaven. One marries whoever God or his agents, the Brahmins, decide upon. Babu Bharatdas had laid down no conditions while seeking a suitable bridegroom for his daughter. But he could not find the kind of boy and family he sought. He wanted his daughter happy, like any dutiful father, but according to him, possessions were of prime importance. Character and education were secondary. Character is not reflected on a person's face and of what value is education in today's world? Of course, if wealth is accompanied by education, then what more can one ask for! He searched far and wide for such a family but in vain. After all, how many families are there with both these attributes? And the few families that did exist were not of the same community. If the community matched, the stars did not; if the stars matched, then the terms and conditions of the marriage could not be agreed upon. Helpless, Bharatdas was forced to get his daughter Leela married off to Lala Santsaran's son, Sitasaran. He was the only son, fairly well-educated, courteous, worldly wise and also quite a romantic at heart. The most important thing was that though he was handsome, strong, cheerful and brave, his views were still very old-fashioned. Whatever was traditional was good, whatever was modern, bad. When it came to business the zamindar used all the new practices for that was an arena where he had no power. But he was a hardcore conservative when it came to societal customs. Sitasaran blindly followed his father in word and deed. He didn't have a mind of his own. A dull intellect often manifests as a lack of social liberalism.

2

Leela's trials started from the day she stepped into the house. The acts that had been encouraged in her own home were prohibited here. Since childhood she had been taught to take in big gulps of air, here it was seen as sinful to even open one's mouth to inhale. As a child she had been taught that sunlight was life, here to even glimpse sunlight was considered harmful. At home, tolerance, forgiveness and compassion were quoted as divine virtues, here one was not free to even name these traits. Santsaran was an extremely acerbic, angry man who wouldn't allow a fly to land on his nose. It was only through cheating and lies that he had amassed so much property. This was his mantra for a successful life. His wife was a notch or two above him. If her *bahu* were ever to be found standing in the doorway of her darkened room or having stepped foot on the terrace, floods would arrive, the heavens would fall. She was stricken with the malady of incessant nagging. A bit of extra salt in the dal was an excuse enough to nag all day.

A huge, hefty woman, laden with jewellery, wearing a wide lehnga of chintz, she sat all day long on her string cot, her box of betel leaves beside her. Even a leaf dared not move against her wish. Observing her bahu's new-fangled habits, she boiled with rage. *Our reputation is at stake. Just look at the way she's peering out from the balcony. If my daughter had such a roving eye, I would have throttled her. Who knows what kind of people live in her part of the world! She never wears any jewellery. Look at her; she couldn't care less about dressing up. Do you think these are good signs?* Not just Leela, Sitasaran too had to face her tongue-lashing. '*Oh, so you also like sleeping in the moonlight, is it? You call yourself a man? What kind of a man is he whose wife does not listen to him? Home all day long, stuck to her. Don't you have a tongue in your head? Why don't you make her understand?*'

Sitasaran would say, 'Amma, if only she would listen.'

'Why won't she listen, aren't you man enough? A mere glance from a man should make a woman tremble.'

'How far have you got trying to make her see reason?'

'You think she cares? She must be thinking—this old woman will die sooner or later and then I will be mistress of this house.'

'Well, what can I say in response to that? Can't you see how weak she has become? She has lost her colour. Her condition is going from bad to worse, being in that room all day long.'

Whenever she heard these words from her son, the mother would smoulder and rage all day long, alternately cursing her luck and this time in her life.

Though he spoke like this in front of his mother, the moment he was with Leela, Sitasaran's attitude would change.

He would say what Leela liked to hear, to such an extent that both made fun of the old woman. Leela had no relief other than this. All through the day she had to do endless chores. She had never sat before a stove, but now she had to slap away at quintals of atta as rotis had to be made for both the workers as well as the errand boys. Sometimes she would sit and weep for hours over the stove. It wasn't as if these people couldn't afford a cook but an old family custom demanded that the bahu cook, and this tradition had to be maintained. It was only the sight of Sitasaran that calmed Leela's tortured spirit momentarily.

One summer evening, a breeze blew outside, but inside it was unbearably stuffy. Leela was sitting and reading a book when Sitasaran came in and said, 'It's very hot in here, sit outside.'

'It is far better to bear this heat than listen to the taunts one would start hearing the moment one steps outside.'

'If she says anything today, I won't be able to hold myself back.'

'And it will then be impossible to even stay in this house.'

'We'll get away from this strife.'

'I won't leave even if it kills me. Whatever she says or does, in her eyes, it's for my own good. It's not as if she has any enmity towards me. Yes, we may not like what she says, but that's a different matter. She herself has had to endure all the suffering that she now wants me to bear. Her suffering has not affected her health in any way. At sixty-five she is sprightlier than me. So how can she comprehend that such suffering might injure one's health?'

Sitasaran looked at her wilted face with beseeching eyes and said, 'You have had to bear much sorrow in this house.

This family is not worthy of you. You must surely have committed some sin in your previous life.'

Playing with her husband's hands, Leela said, 'Then how would I have found your love?'

3

Five years went by. Leela became a mother of two. A boy and a girl. The boy was named Jankisaran and the girl, Kamini. The children kept the house alive. The grandfather doted on the girl, while the grandmother doted on the boy. Both the children were boisterous and spoilt, and were given to cussing and making rude faces. Cussing and making rude faces was nothing to them. They would eat throughout the day and so often fall sick. Leela had tolerated all her own suffering but she could not bear to see these bad habits in her children, but who paid attention to her? Despite the fact that it was she who had given birth to these children, she was not considered significant; the children were everything. She had no right to even scold her own children; her mother-in-law would tear her apart.

The biggest trouble now was that her own health kept getting worse. During her pregnancy she had to undergo all the cruelties that ignorance, foolishness and superstition ordained for child-bearing women. In that hell hole where there was neither air nor light, nor any hygiene, and a foul smell pervaded the musty, filthy room, her delicate form shrivelled up. Whatever fight was left in her after the first childbirth was razed entirely after the second. She became pale and her eyes were sunken hollows. It seemed as if she was bloodless. Her appearance changed completely.

It was summer. There were not just ripe mangoes to eat, but also watermelons. There had never been such a good crop of both fruits. God only knew how they came to be so sweet that year. No one could stop eating them. Baskets laden with mangoes and watermelons arrived from Santsaran's villages. The whole house fell upon them. Babu Sahib was of old stock. In the morning he would breakfast upon a hundred mangoes, then top it up with a full tray of watermelons. The lady of the house did not lag behind. She stopped eating an entire meal. Grain would not spoil after all. If not that day, they would be used another day. But would mangoes and watermelons keep fresh even for a day? You had to eat them all up or let them perish. They were used to this yearly flood of watermelons and mangoes and no one ever complained. If one felt heavy, one simply took some digestive.

One day Sitasaran felt twinges of pain in his tummy. He ignored it and sat down to eat the mangoes. The moment he reached a hundred, he threw up. Collapsed. He had relentless bouts of vomiting and diarrhoea. It was clearly cholera. A doctor was called in from the city but Babu Sahib passed away before he reached. Weeping and the beating of breasts followed. By evening the dead body was carried out of the house. When people returned from the funeral at midnight, the mistress too was found to be suffering from cholera. Once more there was a lot of scurrying around but by sunrise she too was gone. While they lived, husband and wife had not been separated even for a day. In death, too, they left the earth together at the same time. The husband at sunset, and his wife at sunrise.

But the tribulations had not ended. Leela was busy with all the arrangements for the rites, and nobody else bothered about cleaning up the house. On the third day, both the children went into the living room, crying for their grandparents. There was a slice of watermelon and a few mangoes kept on a ledge in the room. Flies were humming over them. Janki climbed on to a stool to reach them and then they sat down to eat them together. By evening both children were struck with cholera; before long their parents were left weeping. The house was enveloped in darkness. Where only three days ago there had been so much clamour, now a pall of gloom had descended; one could not even hear the sound of anyone crying. Who was there to cry? There were only two souls left. And they were too numb to weep.

4

Leela's failing health had made her almost lifeless by now. She didn't have the strength to even get up and sit. She seemed lost all the time, taking no interest either in getting dressed or eating. She appeared to be detached from the home as well as the world outside it. If she sat down somewhere, she would remain sitting. Months went by before she changed her clothes or oiled her hair. The children had been the sole reason for her to live. With them gone, life and death seemed the same. Day and night she prayed to God to rid her of this existence. She had experienced both joy and sorrow; now she had no more desires. But has death ever responded to one's call?

At first Sitasaran too wept a lot every now and then; he would even run away from the house. But as the days passed by, his grief for his children ebbed; it is perhaps the mother who feels the most pain at losing a child to death. Slowly he was able to collect himself. He began to laugh and joke with his friends like before. The ones closest to him would rally around his spirits even more. He was now the master of the house and free to do what he wanted. There was no one to stop him. He began gallivanting all over the place. If once his eyes had welled up with tears at the sight of Leela crying, now he would get irritated looking at her immersed in grief. Life was not meant for crying. God had given them children and it was He who had snatched them away. 'Does that mean that we also give up living?' Leela was shocked to hear this. How could a father utter such words? There seemed to be all kinds of people in this world!

It was the time of Holi. There was much singing and dancing in the men's quarters. A lot of people had been invited for the celebration. Leela was flat on the floor, weeping. She was always reduced to tears when festivals came. If the children had been alive they would have put on new clothes and how they would have romped around! Without them, what festival could they celebrate, what fun could they have?

All at once Sitasaran came in and said, 'Are you going to spend the entire time weeping? Why don't you change your clothes, look more respectable? What have you done to yourself?'

Leela replied, 'You go back to your raucous *mehfil*, what do you care about me.'

'Are you the first to have lost children? Are you the only one to face such tribulations?'

'This we all know. Everyone copes in their own way. How can we control what we feel?'

'Don't you have any duty towards me?'

Leela looked at her husband in bewilderment, clueless about what he meant. Then she averted her face and resumed crying.

'I want to put an end to this gloom. If you don't have any control over your heart, then neither do I. I can't spend my whole life mourning.'

'You go ahead with your fun and games, I'm not stopping you! Why do you stop me from crying?'

'My house is not for weeping.'

'Very well, I will not weep in your house.'

5

Leela could see her husband slipping out of her hands. He had fallen prey to his lust and there was no one who could talk him out of it. He seemed to have lost his senses. She wondered what she could do. If she left, the house would crumble and her husband would be like so many other rich young men trapped in the clutches of his selfish friends. Some slut or the other would enter the house and ruin him completely. *Oh God! What should I do? Were he to fall ill would I forsake him? Never. I would tend to him with all my being, pray to God, plead with the heavenly powers. Agreed that he is not physically ill but he is definitely mentally sick. If a man cries when he has to laugh and laughs when he should be crying, then is there any doubt that he is mad? If I leave him, he will be destroyed. It's my duty to rescue him.*

Yes, I will have to forget my sorrow. Cry I will, for tears are written in my fate—so I will cry but through laughter. I will fight my destiny. I can do little else but cry for those who have gone but I will not let go of those who are present. Oh broken heart! Come, let me gather these pieces and make a grave out of you and surrender my grief to you. Oh tearful eyes, hide my tears behind a halo of laughter. Come, my ornaments, for long have I spurned you, forgive me for this offence. You have been my companion in my good times, on wonderful journeys, now stay with me in this crisis; don't betray me. Leela sat up all night talking to herself, while in the men's quarters it was a total carnival. Drunk out of his senses, Sitasaran would break into song or a fit of clapping. His friends seemed to be painted in the same hue. It seemed that nothing mattered to them but sheer debauchery.

The last mehfil fell silent. No more of their hoo-ha could be heard. Leela wondered whether the crowd had left or fallen asleep. All at once a hush fell over the house. She went and stood at the doorway and peeped into the drawing room. A flame seared through her veins. The friends had departed. No sign of the socialites either. Just a beauty lying on the couch with Sitasaran bent over her, whispering softly into her ear. What was in their minds was clear from their expressions. One's eyes sparkled with interest; the other's leered. Thus is an innocent robbed by maya as beauty incarnate. Leela's possessions were being robbed right under her nose by a bewitching trickster. Leela was so infuriated that she wanted to grab the slut with both hands then and there, snub her so soundly that she would never forget it and throw her out of the house. Those wifely feelings which had lain dormant for so long reawakened and agitated her. But she curbed herself. Surging desires cannot be dammed all of a sudden. She retraced her steps to the house, calmed her mind and thought to herself—*In form and beauty, in feminine wiles, I cannot match this evil one. She's like a piece of the moon, every part of her sparkles, every pore of her is intoxicating. Her eyes are so full of thirst, indeed, not thirst but a volcano!* Leela went right to a mirror. After many months she looked at herself. A sigh escaped her lips. Grief had completely ravaged her body. Next to the seductress she was like a *juhi* flower beside a rose!

6

Sitasaran recovered from his hangover in the evening. When he opened his eyes he saw Leela before him, smiling. His eyes soaked in this rare image of Leela. He felt a thrill, as if he was meeting her after a long separation. How could he know how much she had wept while adorning herself, how many tears she had shed when she wove those flowers into her tresses. With reawakened desire he arose and embraced her. Smiling, he said, 'Today you have adorned yourself with so many weapons that there seems to be nowhere to run.'

Leela laid a finger on her heart and said, 'Stay here. You are always running away, now I will keep you captive. You've enjoyed the pleasures of exotic flowers, now look at the ones inside these dark rooms.'

Shamefaced, Sitasaran said, 'Don't call these dark rooms, Leela! They are overflowing like a divine lake of love.'

Just then, they heard a friend's footsteps outside. As Sitasaran began to walk away, Leela caught his hand and said, 'I won't let you go.'

'I'll be right back.'

'I'm afraid that you will leave me.'

When Sitasaran went outside, his good friend said, 'Did you spend the entire day sleeping? You seem really pleased. We had decided to go there now, right? She is waiting for you.'

'I'm ready to go but Leela won't let me.'

'You're still the same moron. So you're back in your wife's clutches! Then what is it that got you so hot and bothered earlier?'

'Leela had shut me out of the house, so I went here and there seeking refuge. Now she has reopened the gates and is standing at the entrance, calling out to me.'

'Oh come on, how will you find the same pleasure here? No matter how much you adorn the home, can you turn it into a garden?'

'Brother, the home cannot become a garden but it can become heaven. Now I alone know how ashamed I am of my pettiness. She suffered so much grief losing our children that it broke her body and diminished her beauty, and yet she cast it away at just one signal from me. As if this sorrow had never existed in the first place. I know that she can bear a lot of pain. She will protect me above everything else. When she saw that her sorrow was making me suffer, she cast aside her grief entirely. Today when I saw her adorned with ornaments and smiling at me, I was exhilarated. I feel as if she is a Goddess from heaven who has been sent only to protect a weak mortal like me. If I had to sell all my property to take back the cruel words I have uttered to her, I would do it. Truly, Leela is a Goddess from heaven.'

Translated from the Hindi by Swati Pal

The Accusation

Munnu the sweeper cleaned the courtyard and bathroom of Munshi Shyamkishore. After cleaning the house he came to the door and said, 'Maaji, come and see, I have cleaned the whole place. Will I get to eat something today, if you please?'

Devi Rani walked towards the door and said, 'It's not even been ten days since I paid you. You're asking so soon again?'

Munnu asked, 'What can I do, Maaji? It's difficult to meet expenses. A sole man, how do I manage both work and household?'

'Then why don't you get married?' urged Devi.

'You are young right now. For how long will you remain a bachelor?' Devi asked, showing concern.

'You have been taking such good care of me; with your blessings something good will happen. Will you help me?' asked Munnu.

'Yes, I will,' responded Devi. 'You find a girl first. I will do whatever I can.'

'Your temper is very agreeable. You look after me so well. Mistresses in other houses don't even listen or care to talk to us,' Munnu said in a wheedling tone. 'Allah has not only given you a lovely face but also a good heart. Only Allah knows, just by looking at you all my thirst and hunger melt away. I have come across many women from affluent households, but they don't even come close to your sole.'

'You liar! As if I am that beautiful!'

'Now what can I say to you! I see these rich and robust women of big houses, but apart from a fair complexion, they have nothing. They lack this charm, you see.'

'Will one rupee be enough for now?'

'Madam, see if you could spare two rupees.'

Devi gave him the money and said in a tone of dismissal, 'All right, take this and go!'

'Yes, Madam! If you don't mind, can I ask you something?' Munnu asked solicitously.

'What is it, tell me? But quick, I have to go and light the hearth.'

'Then you carry on, please. I will ask some other time,' Munnu prepared to go.

Devi could not help asking, 'No, no. Tell me, what is it? I am not in a hurry.'

Munnu asked her, 'Do you have any relative staying in Dalmandi?'

'No, nobody lives there,' replied Devi.

'Then it must be some friend,' Munnu said rather nonchalantly. 'I usually see your husband walking out of a bungalow.'

'Dalmandi is the locality of prostitutes, no?'

'Yes, Madam, a lot of prostitutes live there, but Sir looks like an innocent man. Does he come back late at night?'

'No, he is back before evening and doesn't go anywhere after that. Though sometimes he goes to the library . . .' she said nervously.

'All right, so that must be it, right?' remarked Munnu. 'If you get a chance, then caution him not to visit that place at night. No matter how pure a person is at heart, onlookers will always be suspicious.'

By then Babu Shyamkishore had arrived. Munnu greeted him, picked up his bucket and left.

Shyamkishore asked, 'What was Munnu saying?'

'Nothing, he was just going on about himself. He was asking for food. I gave him two rupees. He speaks quite cordially.'

'You are extremely talkative! If you find no one else, then let it be this sweeper. How can you talk to this fool?' Shyam hissed at her.

'As if I like looking at his face! He's a poor man. How can I turn my back if he starts crying about his fate?' Devi hissed back.

Babu Sahib unfolded a garland of jasmine flowers from his handkerchief and put it around Devi's neck, but there was no sign of joy on her face. She looked at him from the corner of her eye and said, 'You like to stroll in Dalmandi quite often these days, isn't it?'

Shyam asked surprised, 'Who? Me?'

'Oh yes, you. You make an excuse of going to the library here, but it's all about the fun you have there!'

Shyam made a disgusted face, 'All lies! Complete rubbish. Who told you all this? This Munnu?'

'Munnu didn't tell me anything; I am aware of all your whereabouts,' she said defensively.

'You don't need to keep an eye on me. Suspicion is a great folly and if you get into this habit, major tragedies can befall. Why would I go to Dalmandi? Do I have someone better off in Dalmandi than you? I am a lover of your intoxicating eyes. Even if a nymph stands before me, I won't care to notice her. Where is Sharda today?'

'She has gone to play downstairs.'

'Just don't let her go outside. Cars and carriages are always on the move,' his tone was a little thoughtful. 'Who knows what can happen! Just today there was an accident at Ardali Bazar. Three boys were crushed.'

Devi exclaimed, scandalized, 'Three boys! That's catastrophic. Whose vehicle was it?'

'That is not known yet.' He added quickly, 'God knows, these flowers look beautiful on you.'

Devi smiled coyly, 'Come now, stop this flattery!'

After three days, Munnu said to Devi, 'Madam, talks are on about my betrothal. I have full faith in you and I am going ahead with it.'

Devi asked, 'Have you seen the girl? How is she?'

'It will be as destined. At least I will get to eat home-made rotis now, otherwise I had to cook on my own,' moaned Munnu. 'Thankfully she has a gentle nature. Women in our community are quite frivolous, Madam! It's hard to find a pious one in a crowd of hundred.'

'You people don't say anything to your women?'

'What can we say, Madam! We are scared stiff as they complain to our bosses and get us dismissed. Babus keep an eye on these sweeper-women, Madam.'

Devi giggled, 'You liar! Are the wives of babus much worse than these sweeper-women?'

'Now, Madam, don't make me say it,' said Munnu. 'I have not seen anyone who can match your impassioned speech. I am a small man, Madam, but had my wife been like the wives of these babus, then even I wouldn't have felt like talking to them. I haven't really come across anyone with a face like yours.'

'Oh, you fibber, where did you learn all this sweet talk?'

Wondering if he had underestimated her, Munnu continued, 'This is no sweet talk, Madam; I speak the truth. You were standing in front of the window one day. Raza Miyan's glance fell upon you. He is the owner of a big shoe shop. Allah has bestowed him with wealth and heart alike! He lowered his eyes the moment he saw you. Today, while talking to me, he began to sing praises of your face. I said, "Allah has given her a face as beautiful as her heart."'

Devi asked, 'All right, is he that tall, dusky young man?'

Munnu confirmed, 'Yes, Madam, that's him. He said to me that if only he could get another glimpse of you, but I scolded him and said, "Don't you dare speak to me like that. You don't have a chance here."'

'You did the right thing. May that blockhead lose his eyes!' cried Devi. 'Whenever he passes by, his eyes are always on the window. Let him know that he better not raise his eyes here.'

Munnu reassured her, 'I have already said that, Madam; now I should leave. Is there anything else to be cleaned? It's time for sir to come home. If he sees me here, he will say, "What nonsense is he talking again?"'

Devi pleaded, 'Take these rotis. This will save you from the effort of cooking today.'

Munnu went away murmuring, 'May Allah keep you safe! I feel like staying close to this door and eating whatever crumbs come my way. Seriously, the moment I see you, my hunger and thirst disappear.'

Munnu was just leaving when Munshi Shyamkishore arrived upstairs. His last sentence reached his ears. As soon as Munnu left, Babu Sahib said to Devi, 'I had asked you not to entertain Munnu, but you don't listen to me. People like him take the news of one house to another; one should never talk to these people. What was that about hunger and thirst disappearing?'

Devi mumbled, 'I don't know, what hunger and thirst? There wasn't any such talk.'

'How is that so? I clearly heard it myself,' he said sharply.

Devi replied in an exhausted voice, 'I don't seem to remember. Must be something. As if I sit and listen to everything he says.'

Shyam said reproachfully, 'Then does he talk to the walls? Listen, there is a man who just passed by, looking towards the window. A Muslim lad from this neighbourhood. He runs a shoe shop. Why do you keep standing near the window?'

'The shutters are drawn,' cried Devi.

Shyam said impatiently, 'Even if you stand behind the shutters, any man can clearly see you.'

'I didn't know that. Now I won't open the window at all.'

'Yes, what's the use? Don't let Munnu come inside,' he pleaded.

Devi turned her head and asked, 'But who will clean the bathroom?'

Shyam said, 'Well, he can come but don't talk to him much. A new theatre has come to town today. Let's go and watch it. I've heard that the actors are quite good.'

At this moment, Sharda came running with a box of sweets. Devi asked her, 'Hey, who gave you these sweets?'

'Raja Bhaiya gave them to me. He says that he will buy me new toys,' responded Sharda.

Shyam asked her, 'Who is Raja Bhaiya?'

Sharda replied coolly, 'The same man who just passed by.'

'Is that man tall and dusky?' Shyam hissed.

'Yes, yes! That's him. Can I go to his house every day?' Sharda asked excitedly.

Devi asked, 'Did you go to his house?'

Sharda said with a sudden grin, 'He lifted me in his arms and took me to his place.'

Shyam snapped, 'Don't you play on the road downstairs. You will come under a car someday. Don't you see, so many cars speed past!'

'Raja Bhaiya says that he will take me for a ride in his car to get some fresh air.'

'What do you do all day long? Can't you keep an eye on your own girl?' Shyam asked hotly.

Devi snapped at him, 'A girl this big cannot be kept locked in a trunk.'

'You are quick when it comes to answering back. Why don't you admit that you don't find the time because you keep talking all the while?'

'Whom do I talk to?' Devi looked at him scornfully. 'There aren't even any neighbours around.'

'But there is Munnu,' hissed Shyam.

Devi bit her lip and said, 'Is Munnu my relative that I will sit and talk to him? He's a poor man who cries about his fate. What am I supposed to say? I can't chide him.'

'Anyway, prepare the food, the performance will start at nine o'clock. It's seven already,' said Shyam.

'You go and watch it,' she announced. 'I won't go.'

'You were the one who kept telling me for months that you wanted to watch the play. Now what's wrong?' cried Shyam. 'Have you taken a vow that you will oppose whatever I say?'

Devi replied weakly, 'I don't know why you think this way. I do everything according to your wishes. If I go, you will end up spending more money and then say that your expenses have increased and badger me no end. That's why I said it. If you want me to come, then I can. Who doesn't like to watch a play?'

At nine o'clock, Shyamkishore, along with Devi and Sharda, left for the theatre in a tonga. They had barely started when another tonga appeared from behind. Raza was in it. And next to him—yes, Munnu the sweeper who used to clean Babu Sahib's house was seated next to him. Devi lowered her head on seeing them. She was shocked to see that Raza and Munnu were such good friends that Raza took him in his tonga for a ride. Sharda saw Raza and cried at once, 'Babuji, look, that's Raja Bhaiya coming.' She clapped her hands and called out excitedly, 'Raja Bhaiya, look here, we are going to watch a play.'

Raza smiled, and Babu Sahib boiled with rage. He thought that these nasty people were here to follow him. *There was definitely some secret understanding between the two. Otherwise why would Raza bring Munnu along?* To put them off their pursuit, he said to his tonga driver, 'Be quick, we are getting late.' The tonga picked up speed. Raza's tonga also started racing ahead. When Babu Sahib asked the tonga driver to slow down, Raza too slowed down. Finally, Babu Sahib said in exasperation, 'Take the tonga towards the cantonment, we won't go to the theatre.'

The tonga driver looked at him questioningly and turned the tonga. Raza too took a turn. Babu Sahib was so filled with rage that he was about to challenge Raza, but he feared picking up a fight which would attract an unnecessary crowd and could turn serious. He controlled himself. He got irritated with himself for having chosen to watch the play. He had no clue that these devils would follow him. *I will get rid of Munnu tomorrow itself,* he thought. Raza's tonga turned in a different direction after going a certain distance, and Babu Sahib's anger slowly subsided, but it was too late to go to the theatre now. They rode back home from the cantonment.

Devi reached upstairs and hissed irritatedly, 'The tonga driver earned two rupees for nothing!'

Shyamkishore gave her a bloodshot stare and exclaimed, 'Talk to Munnu some more, enjoy looking at Raza from the window. What exactly are you up to?'

Devi raised her voice angrily, 'Aren't you ashamed to say such things? You are insulting me unnecessarily, this won't be good for you. I don't even consider anyone equal to the dirt on your feet, then who the hell is that sweeper? You think I am so low?'

Shyam replied curtly, 'No, I don't consider you so, but I do think you're a fool. You should never have entertained this rogue at all. Now do you see what a rascal he is, or do you still have your doubts?'

Devi muttered under her breath, 'I will get rid of him tomorrow itself.'

Munshiji lay down with an unsettled mind. He was in his office all day long. How could he know what Devi did behind his back? He knew that Devi was a devoted wife, but he also knew that women have a habit of showing off their beauty. Devi must be appearing at the window all decked up, and these scoundrels in the colony must be getting ideas in their heart of hearts. It was beyond him to stop this business. These rogues are clever at seduction. God forbid that their eyes fall upon the brides and daughters of respectable families! How to get rid of them?

After giving it careful thought, he decided to leave that house. He couldn't think of anything else. He asked Devi, 'So tell me, should we leave this house? I fear that they will sully my name if we stay amidst these rogues.'

Devi spoke in a challenging tone, 'As you wish!'

Shyam asked her again, 'You only tell me the way out.'

Devi sputtered, 'What can I say? I don't think we need to leave the house even if there were to be a lakh of such scoundrels, let alone one or two. Is one supposed to leave his house because of a few barking dogs?'

'Sometimes, the dogs can bite too,' Shyam warned her.

Devi didn't respond to this remark. She was afraid that arguing over this would arouse her husband's suspicion further. He was anyway suspicious by nature; who knows what he might think of her answer!

Shyam Babu left that house three days after the incident.

One day, a month after shifting into the new house, Munnu, with a bandage around his head, came limping with a stick and called out. Devi recognized his voice, but did not reproach him. She opened the door. She was yearning to hear some news about her old house. Munnu came inside and said, 'Madam, ever since you've left that house, I swear, not once have I gone there. I feel like crying when I see that house. I wish I could come to this colony. I keep roaming here and there like a madman, Madam, I don't feel like doing anything. I keep thinking of you all the time. Who will look after me the way you did? This house is quite small.'

Devi replied firmly, 'We had to leave that house because of you.'

Munnu exclaimed in shock, 'Because of me? What did I do, Madam?'

'You were the one who was following us with Raza in the tonga. Anyone would be suspicious of such a man,' groaned Devi.

Munnu feigned pulling himself together and said, 'Oh, Madam, do not speak of that night. Raza Miyan had to meet a lawyer. He stays in the cantonment. He asked me to accompany him. His horse-wrangler had gone somewhere. Out of regard, we couldn't overtake you. You call him a scoundrel, but there isn't a kinder man in the entire colony. He prays five times a day, Madam, fasts for all thirty days. He has his wife and children at home. He dare not misbehave with anyone.'

'Anyway, must be. Why is your head bandaged?'

Munnu cried in an aggrieved tone, 'Don't ask me about it, Madam! My blood boils with rage when I hear people saying anything bad about you. The confectioner who stays next door was saying, "Babuji has yet to give me some money." I said, "He is not the sort of person who will keep your money with him." That's it, Madam. On that note, he picked up a fight with me. I was cleaning the drain beneath the shop. He came down and kicked me hard. I fell flat on the road. I got hurt, but I abused him so much that he will remember it for the rest of his life. The wound is healing now, Madam.'

Devi cried anxiously, 'Ram Ram! Why did you pick a fight for nothing? It was a simple matter. You should have said, "If he owes you money, then why don't you go and ask for it." We are in the same town; it's not like we have fled the country.'

'Madam, I cannot stand anyone speaking against you. I don't care if he is the owner of his house, how do I care?' Munnu said resolutely. 'Even if he is a moneylender, he must be so in his own house. As if we eat from his share.'

Devi asked him, 'Has someone moved into that house yet?'

Munnu burst out in agony, 'Many people came to see the house, Madam, but a house in which you have stayed, how can someone else live there? We have told them to keep away from the house. Raza has not touched food and water ever since you've left, Madam. He cries thinking of your daughter. But why would you think of poor people like us?'

'Why wouldn't I? Am I not a human being?' Devi gave him a pitying look. 'Even animals don't eat for three to four days after leaving their old habitat. Take this money, go and buy something from the bazaar to eat, you must be hungry.'

Munnu said eagerly, 'With your blessings, there is no shortage of food. A person's heart is all that matters, Madam! Money has nothing to do with it. We eat because you feed us. Your temperament is such that a man can slave away without taking a penny from you. I will take your leave now, Madam. Sir must be on his way. He'll say, "The rascal has come here too."'

'He will take time to come,' responded Devi.

Munnu said quickly, 'Oh, I forgot to tell you this. Raza Miyan has given these toys for the little girl. I got so engrossed in the conversation that I totally forgot. Where is she?'

'She isn't back from school yet, but what was the need to send so many toys? Oh, what has Raza done! He should have sent toys worth two or three rupees if he wanted to. This doll alone must be worth at least four rupees. These toys are worth thirty to thirty-five rupees.'

'How would I know, Madam? I have never bought any toys. Even if there're worth thirty-five rupees, it's not a huge amount for him. He earns a daily profit of fifty rupees from his shop, Madam!'

'No, take them back, please,' Devi protested. 'What will she do with so many toys? Let me just keep this doll.'

Munnu tried cajoling her, 'Madam, Raza Miyan will be disappointed. He won't spare me. He's a very sentimental man, Madam. He becomes restless when his wife leaves for her hometown for even a day or two.'

All at once, Sharda returned from school and pounced on the toys as soon as she saw them. Devi scolded her and hissed, 'What are you doing? Take the doll, what will you do with all others?'

Sharda could not contain her joy. 'I will take all of them. I will keep the doll in the car and take her for a ride. The dog will run after them. I will cook for my doll in these utensils. Where did all this come from, Amma? Tell me.'

'They haven't come from anywhere. I had asked for them just to have a look. You choose any one of them,' Devi said drily.

'I will take all of them, Amma, please take all of them,' pleaded Sharda. 'Who has brought them, Amma?'

Devi raised her voice, 'Munnu, you take the toys and leave! Let the doll remain.'

Sharda continued to lament, 'Where have you brought these from, Munnu, tell me!'

'Your Raja Bhaiya has sent them for you,' said Munnu.

Sharda was overcome with joy. 'Raja Bhaiya has sent them. Oh! (dances) Raja Bhaiya is very nice. I will show these to my friends tomorrow. No one has such toys.'

Devi said to Munnu, 'All right, Munnu, you go now. Tell Raza Miyan not to send any more toys again.'

After Munnu left, Devi called Sharda, 'Come, child, let me put the toys away. If Babuji sees them he will get annoyed about you taking these toys from Raza Miyan. He will break and throw all of them away. Don't ever mention the toys to him.'

'Yes, Amma, keep them away. Babuji will destroy them,' Sharda said rather sadly.

Devi alerted her again, 'Don't ever let him know that Raja Bhaiya sent these toys, otherwise Babuji will hit Raja Bhaiya and will also box your ears. He will say that this girl keeps begging for toys from everyone.'

Sharda repeated, 'Yes, Amma, keep them away. Babuji will break them.'

By then, Babu Shyamkishore came back from the office. He had a frown on his face. As soon as he entered, he howled, 'That rogue Munnu has started coming to this colony as well? I saw him today. Did he come here too?'

Devi said hesitantly, 'Well, yes.'

Shyam's face was distorted with anger, 'And you let him in? Didn't I ask you not to let him step inside the house again?'

'He started knocking on the door, what was I supposed to do?' said Devi.

'That rascal must have come with him too?' Shyam snapped.

'There was no one with him!' she said.

Shyam gave her a questioning glance. 'You did not tell him not to come here again, did you?'

'I didn't think of this. And why will he come here again?' she said meekly.

Shyam reminded her, 'For the same reason he came today. Why are you hell-bent on ruining my reputation?'

Devi spoke with attitude, rather annoyed, 'Don't you give me this nonsense, understand? Aren't you ashamed of yourself for speaking such filth? You had said something similar before. Today you're saying it again. If I hear this for the third time, it won't be good. I am warning you. You think I'm a whore?'

'I don't want him to come to my house,' protested Shyam.

Devi retorted, 'Then why don't you tell him yourself? Do I stop you?'

Shyam hissed, 'Why don't you tell him?'

She could not bring herself to ignore this remark. 'Are you ashamed to tell him yourself?'

Shyam said, 'It is pointless for me to tell him. Even if I ask him not to come, he will keep coming unless you ask him to stop.'

Devi bit her lip and said, 'All right, what is the harm if he keeps coming? Sweepers go to everyone's house.'

'If I see Munnu here again, it won't be good for you, I've warned you.'

Saying this, Shyamkishore went downstairs. Devi stood there, benumbed. She was hurt after facing this accusation, disgrace and mistrust. She began to cry. The thing which had hurt her most was the fact that her husband considered her so lowly and salacious. He was suspecting her of something that even a whore wouldn't do.

The moment Shyamkishore entered the house, Sharda collected her toys and ran off lest he destroy them. She went downstairs and started looking for a place to hide them. She was in this quandary when one of her friends came to the courtyard. Sharda was impatient to show off her toys. She could not overcome this temptation. Babuji went upstairs, he will not come down so soon. Till then, why not show the toys to my friend? She called out to her friend and both of them got so engrossed in looking at the new toys that they didn't realize when Shyamkishore came downstairs. As soon as Shyamkishore saw the toys, he went to Sharda and asked, 'Where did you get these toys?'

Sharda choked at once. She started trembling with fear and couldn't utter a word.

Shyamkishore blustered and asked her again, 'Why don't you speak, who gave you these toys?'

Sharda started crying. Cajoling her, Shyamkishore said, 'Don't cry, I won't beat you. I am just asking you, where did you get these pretty toys?'

When he assured her thus three or four times, Sharda gained some courage. She told him the entire story. Catastrophe! It would have been better had Sharda stayed mum. In fact, way better if she had turned mute. Devi could have cooked up a story to avoid this situation, but who could avert the inevitable? Every inch of Shyamkishore was on fire. Leaving the toys behind, he went upstairs and, holding Devi by her shoulders, asked her, 'Do you want to stay in this house or not? Tell me clearly.'

Devi was still standing and sobbing. Hearing this ruthless question, her tears simply vanished. Fearing a new menace, she forgot about the previous accusations. It was like a patient running away from his sickbed upon seeing a slayer's sword. She looked at Shyamkishore with fear-stricken eyes, but couldn't say anything. Every mute cell of her body was asking him, 'What is the meaning of this question?'

Shyamkishore asked again, 'You clearly let me know what you want. If you're tired of living with me, then you are free to go. I don't want to imprison you. You don't have to lie to me or cheat on me. I am ready to dismiss you happily. If you have decided something, then so have I. You cannot live in this house any more; you don't deserve to live here.'

Devi gained control of her voice and said, 'What has happened to you these days that you keep spitting venom all the time? If you're tired of me, then poison me. Why do you have to incinerate me? Talking to a sweeper was not that great a crime. When he called out, I went and opened the door. Had I known that this small thing would be blown out of proportion, I would have asked him to go back from afar.'

Shyam cried wildly, 'I wish I could pull out your tongue from your mouth. It began with talking, then communicating through gestures, and now the gifts have also started coming. Now what else is left?'

Devi called out weakly, 'Why are you behaving so ruthlessly? You won't get anything by taking the life of a helpless woman.'

'Am I lying?' asked Shyam.

Devi said, 'Yes, you are.'

Shyam burst out, 'Where did these toys come from?'

Devi's heart almost stopped beating. Her body wouldn't bleed if dissected. She understood that the stars were not in her favour at the moment; devastation seemed likely. *At what inauspicious hour did these toys come in! Why did I take them? I should have returned them right then!* She tried parrying and said, 'To hell with those toys! How could I stop the child, she didn't listen to me! I kept saying, don't take them, but she refused to listen. What else could have I done! But had I known that these toys would cost me my life, I would have snatched and thrown them away.'

Shyam asked gravely, 'What else has come with them? Let me know for your own good.'

'Whatever has come should be in the house. Why don't you check for yourself? It isn't that big a house that it should take you four days to search,' Devi stood murmuring curtly.

Shyam's voice became aggressive. 'I don't have that much free time. It's better that you bring whatever has come. It's highly unlikely that no gift has been sent for you along with these toys. Even if you swore on the Ganga, I wouldn't believe it.'

'Then why don't you search the house?'

Shyamkishore clenched his fist and said, 'I've told you that I don't have the time. Just bring out all the things, otherwise I will strangle you this very moment.'

'Kill me if you want to; how can I show you things which have not come in the first place?'

Hysterically, Shyamkishore pushed her with such force that she fell flat on the ground. He placed his hands around her throat and yelled, 'Should I strangle you to death? Will you not show me the stuff?'

'Fulfil all your wishes.'

'I'll drink your blood. Who do you think I am?'

'If that's what will make your heart contented, then drink it.'

Shyam bawled at her, 'Will you talk to that sweeper again? The next time I see Munnu or that rascal on my threshold, I will slit your throat.'

Saying this, Shyamkishore let go of Devi and walked out of the house. But Devi remained in that state for a long time. There was no trace of love for her husband at that moment. Her soul was uneasily seeking revenge. Perhaps she would have felt happy if someone, at that time, had beaten up Shyamkishore in the bazaar with shoes. After getting thwacked for so many days, this bitter wind had brought down the wall of love, and there was nothing left to console the heart. Today, there was only a thin thread of hesitation and worldly shame that could just break any moment.

When Shyamkishore left, Sharda also went outside the house with her toys. Babuji didn't say anything after seeing the toys, so what was there to worry about! Now, why wouldn't she show her toys to her friends? There was a sweet shop right across the road. The confectioner's daughter was standing next to the door. Sharda started to show her the toys. There was a road in the middle that was busy with traffic. Sharda was oblivious to the world, unaware of its dangers. She ran in a childlike exuberance with her toys.

Little did she know that death was also approaching her to play the game of life and eternal rest. A car was coming from one side and a carriage from the other. Sharda ran, thinking that she would cross the road. The car honked; Sharda fled at her top speed to cross the road, but who could prevent fate! The car crushed her and sped away. She became a mangled piece of flesh, lying on the road, while the toys were left untouched. None of them had been broken! The toys were left behind, the one who played with them had gone. Who was mortal amongst the two, who was to decide!

People rushed in from all the corners. 'Oh, this is Babuji's daughter who stays on the first floor.' Who was to lift the corpse? A man leapt upstairs and called out, 'Babuji! Was your daughter playing down on the road? Please come and see.'

Devi looked down from her terrace. Sharda's body was lying on the road. She shrieked and rushed out to pick her up. Her legs were shaking. This bolt left her almost paralysed. She couldn't even shed a tear.

People in the colony began to ask, 'Where has Babuji gone? How to call him?'

What could Devi say? She was nearly unconscious. Taking the dead body in her lap, drenched with her daughter's blood, she looked up fixedly towards the sky, as if asking the Almighty, 'Am I to bear all the disasters?'

It was getting dark, but there was no news of Babuji. She didn't even know where he had gone. It was nine o'clock, but Babuji didn't return. He was never out for so long. Did he have to vanish today of all days? It was ten o'clock by then, and Devi began to cry. She was sadder at her helplessness than at her daughter's death. How was she supposed to cremate her? Who would go with her? Would anyone be ready to go with her at this late hour? If nobody came forward, then would she have to go on her own? Would the body remain here the whole night?

The darker it got, the more Devi began to fear. She regretted not having taken the body in the evening itself.

It was eleven o'clock. Suddenly someone opened the door. Devi stood up. She thought Babuji had come back.

Her heart began to pound. Crying, she went out. However, it wasn't Babuji, but some policemen who had come to investigate the incident. The accident had occurred at five o'clock. The investigation was held at eleven. After all, the officer-in-charge was also a human being; he too went out for stroll in the evenings.

The inquiry went on for about an hour. Devi understood that diffidence wouldn't do. Whatever the inspector asked her, she replied nonchalantly. She didn't show any sign of shyness or fear. The officer-in-charge was also surprised.

When he was about to leave after recording her statement, Devi inquired, 'Will you be able to find out about that car?'

The constable replied nervously, 'It is highly unlikely that we will get any information about that car.'

'So there will be no punishment for the culprit?' Devi asked in a state of bewilderment.

The constable said, 'It's a constraint. Nobody knows the number.'

Devi probed further, 'Can't the government do something about it? Will the children of poor people continue to perish like this?'

The constable again conveyed his helplessness, 'What can be done? Cars won't just stop plying.'

'At least the policemen should ensure that vehicles don't speed at this rate in the city. But why will you people look into this?' Devi said sharply. 'You officers too sit in these cars. If you begin to stop these cars, then how will you continue to serve?'

The constable left, ashamed. When they reached the road, one of them said, 'This lady has quite an attitude!'

The other constable went on casually, 'Oh man, this woman has left me speechless. What a fine beauty she is! But

I swear, I did not look at her. I couldn't pluck up the courage to stare!'

It was past midnight when Babu Shyamkishore came back, drunk. He had got the news on the way. He stepped inside the house crying. Devi was sitting, incensed. She had made up her mind, 'Whatever may happen, I will rebuke him for sure.' But the moment she saw him crying, all her anger disappeared. She herself started crying. Both of them wept for a long time. This incident had drawn them closer than ever before. They felt that the old romance had been rekindled between them.

Early next morning, when people returned after the cremation, Shyamkishore looked at Devi lovingly and said in a melancholic tone, 'How will you spend your time alone now?'

Devi pleaded, 'Can't you take leave for five or ten days?'

Shyam assured her, 'This is what I was also thinking. I'll apply for leave.'

Shyam Babu went off to take leave from his office. Even during this hardship, Devi's heart was brimming with happiness. After losing her daughter, she had regained the love and trust of her husband, and this was enough to wipe away her tears. However, destiny had its own plans. Ah! Unlucky woman! Do not be happy. The final catastrophe is yet to strike, and you can't even imagine what that can be.

The next day, Babu Shyamkishore was at home when Munnu came and offered a salute. Shyamkishore asked him in a rather stern voice, 'What is it? Why do you come here often?'

Munnu said humbly, 'Sir, whoever hears about yesterday will be filled with sadness. I have been your slave, after all.

So what if I don't work for you? I have been your loyal servant. Can that ever be forgotten? I have come to see if you are doing okay. I can't tell you how miserable I've been feeling ever since I heard about yesterday. Such a sweet girl she was, I forgot all my worries whenever I saw her. The moment she saw me, she would come out running and shout, "Munnu, Munnu"; when we as outsiders can feel this way, I can't even imagine what must be going through your mind.'

Shyam Babu softened a little and said, 'What can a man do against the will of God? My home is filled with darkness. I don't feel like staying here any more.'

Munnu asked, 'Madam must be feeling even more miserable.'

Shyam said drily, 'She is. I used to play with Sharda sometimes but she used to be with her all day long. I can even manage to stop thinking in the midst of work. But how can she? It's a lifelong misery for her.'

Hearing her husband talk to Munnu, Devi peered at the courtyard from the terrace. Seeing Munnu, her eyes welled with tears. She cried out, 'Munnu, I have been devastated!'

Munnu expressed his sympathy, 'Control yourself, Madam. What's the use of crying? It's because of all these misfortunes that one is compelled to deem Allah as cruel. People who are dishonest continue to thrive, even Allah fears them. However, people who are honest and innocent have to bear all the hardships.'

Munnu kept on consoling Devi. Shyam Babu was also rooting for all that Munnu was saying. When he left, Babu Sahib said, 'He doesn't seem to be a bad person.'

Devi echoed agreeably, 'He's an affectionate man. Had he not felt sad, why would he have cared to come?'

Fifteen days passed. Babu Sahib started attending office. Munnu didn't come again. Till now, Devi would kill time by talking to her husband, but now that he had resumed his duties, she would often miss Sharda. She usually spent her days crying. A few low-caste women staying in the same colony used to visit her sometimes but Devi couldn't find any solace in them. They wanted to get something out of her after showing their false sympathies.

One day, around four o'clock, Munnu came again and called out from the courtyard, 'Madam, it's me, Munnu. Can you please come down?'

Devi asked him from upstairs, 'What is it? Tell me.'

'Please come.'

Devi came down and Munnu said, 'Raza Miyan is standing outside. He is here to offer his condolences to you.'

'Go and tell him it was all God's wish.'

Raza was standing at the door. He heard this exchange clearly. He spoke from where he stood, 'The Almighty knows, ever since I've heard this news, my heart has been smashed to smithereens. I had gone to Delhi for some work. I came back today. Had this happened in my presence, what could have I done? But I wouldn't have spared that vehicle-owner, even if he were a king. I would have scoured the whole city. Babu Sahib just gave up and slept over it; that's not done. Can anyone just run over someone and take his life! That cruel person has killed a delicate, sweet girl. Oh! Now who will call me Raja Bhaiya! I swear to God, I have brought a bagful of toys for her. But how was I to know that this misfortune had happened here. Munnu, here, take this amulet and give it to madam. She can tie it in her bun. If God wills, she will be saved from all the dangers henceforth. She must be having nightmares, she mustn't be getting proper sleep, her heart must always be full and heavy. This amulet will ease her maladies. I have got it from a well-known dervish.'

For a long time Munnu and Raza did not budge from the door till they saw Babu Sahib coming their way. Shyamkishore saw them leaving. He went upstairs and asked sternly, 'Why did Raza come here?'

Devi replied meekly, 'He had come to offer his condolences; he has come back from Delhi today. He came here after hearing the news.'

'Men offer condolences to men, not women!' Shyam threw a curt remark.

Devi said, 'You weren't here, so he expressed his concerns to me and left.'

Shyam was again overcome with restlessness, 'So this means that if someone comes to meet me, he can meet you instead if I am not available. There is no problem in that, right?'

'I am not going to meet all of them,' Devi murmured sadly.

Shyam snapped at her, 'So is Raza my brother-in-law or my father-in-law?'

'Why do you become agitated by the smallest of matters?'

'Is this is a small matter? A woman from a respectable family talking to a rogue, is it a small matter? Then what is a big matter? Is it a small matter if I strangle you to death and be spared from the sin? I can very well see that you're back to where it all began. You don't seem to realize even after getting such a huge punishment. Do you want to take my life now?'

Devi was lulled into silence. On the one hand, the grief of losing her daughter, and on the other, the bombardment of abuse and accusations! She felt dizzy. She sat down and began to cry. 'Death is far better than leading such a life!' She could only utter this.

Enraged, Babu Sahib said, 'Don't you worry, this is what will happen. If you want to die, then even I don't expect you to be immortal. It's better for you to die as soon as possible. At least my kin shall be saved from this disgrace.'

Devi said sobbing, 'Why do you misjudge a poor woman? Do you really feel nothing for me?'

'Shut up, I tell you!'

'Why should I shut up? Can you keep me tongue-tied?'

'Again you're going on and on! I will get up and smash your head.'

'Will you? Really?'

'All right then, let us see who your well-wishers are. Call them.'

Saying this, Babu Shyamkishore got up and slapped Devi several times and kicked her, but she didn't cry, nor did she shout or utter a single word. She simply kept staring at him with vacant eyes, as if to decide whether he was a man or something else.

When Shyamkishore had pulled away, Devi said, 'If you are not contented, then you can hit me again. Perhaps you will not get another chance.'

Shyamkishore answered, 'I will chop off your head! What do you think of yourself?'

Saying this, he went downstairs and banged open the door, clanged it shut and walked off. A river of tears started flowing from Devi's eyes.

It was ten o'clock, but Shyamkishore had not returned. Devi's eyes were swollen from all the crying. All her sweet memories had disappeared in the fury. It seemed to Devi that Shyamkishore had never loved her. Yes, he had sung praises of her beauty in the past few days, but that was all made up. It was to enjoy the bloom of her youth that he did all that sweet talk, that he hugged her and laid her on his chest. It was all a façade, only playacting. She couldn't recall if she was ever truly loved by him. Now she did not have her beauty, or her youth or freshness. So why would he not treat her badly? *Now he is bored of me, otherwise why would he pounce on me for every little thing? He wants to get rid of me by blaming me for something or the other. If that is the case, then why should I stay in his house? Just to cook for him or become the victim of his wretchedness? When there is no love, there is no point in my staying here! If nothing else, at least I won't be treated like this in my own house. If he wants this, then so be it. I will think that I have become a widow.*

As night approached, Devi began to feel more terrified. She was worried that he would return and beat her again. He had left seething with anger. *Oh, my destiny! Does he think me to be so low that I will have affairs with sweepers and shoemakers? This man is not even ashamed to say such things! I don't know how he thinks of all this. It's just that he himself is a lowly creature, a typical, selfish person. One should behave in a lowly fashion with such lowly people. It was my fault to have put up with his rash behaviour. Where there is no respect, no limits, no love and no trust, it is worthless to stay in such a place. I've not been sold off to him that he can do anything with me, cut me or thrash me, and I will keep suffering in silence. If there were wives like Sita, then there were husbands like Ram too!*

Devi started feeling fearful that Shyamkishore would actually kill her when he came back, or stab her with a knife.

She had read of such cases in the newspaper. There had been such incidents within the city too. She shuddered with fear. She felt that her life was in danger.

Devi packed her clothes in a small bundle and started thinking. *How do I get out of here? And then where do I go? If I knew where Munnu lived, that would have been of great help. He would have taken me to my house.* She just wanted to reach her home. *Then she would not think of coming back even if her husband cried or banged his head on the wall. He too would regret it! Why should she leave the money? So that he could make merry? I have saved this money with much difficulty. As if he has great savings. Had I spent all this, there would have been nothing left. I used to save up so much.*

Devi went downstairs and locked the door. Then she took out all her jewellery and money, and placed them safely in her bundle. All the money was in notes, so it wasn't too heavy.

Suddenly, someone banged on the door. Devi was startled. She peeked from above, it was Shyam Babu. She couldn't muster the courage to open the door. Just then, Babu Sahib started banging on the door violently as if to break it open. The way he was banging was enough indication of his state of mind. Devi could not dare to face this danger.

In the end, Shyamkishore shouted, 'Damn it, open the door. You bloody . . . ! Open the door, right now!'

Devi lost whatever little courage she had. Shyamkishore was high on liquor. Had he come back sober, he would have softened a little. *I won't open the door, let him break it open. Now you won't find me in this house, so how will you hit me? I've seen your true colours.*

After shouting and banging on the door for another fifteen minutes, Shyamkishore began to talk nonsense. A few neighbours also shouted back at him, 'Despite being an educated man, you come home after midnight! After all, it is a matter of sleep; if she doesn't wake up, then what can be done? Go and sleep at a friend's place tonight, come back in the morning.'

After Shyamkishore left, Devi took her bundle and went downstairs with light steps. She stood near the door for a while to confirm that Shyamkishore had left. When she was sure he had left, she quietly opened the door and walked out. She wasn't angry or sad. She was only eager to run away from this place. She had no one she could trust or who could be of any help to her at this time of adversity. There was only the sweeper Munnu. All her hopes were now pinned on finding him. She would only be able to decide when she met him. Now she wasn't keen on going home. She was afraid that she wouldn't be able to get rid of Shyamkishore if she were to go there. On not finding her here, he would definitely go to her house and bring her back forcefully. She was willing to bear every torture and insult, but did not want to see Shyamkishore again. Love, when spurned, turns into hatred.

There was a crossroads in the vicinity where many tongas were waiting. Devi hired one of them and asked the driver to go to the station.

Devi spent the night at the station. Early in the morning, she hired a tonga and reached the crossroads incognito. The shops had not opened yet, but she inquired about Raza Miyan's address. A boy was sweeping the floor of his shop. Devi called him and said, 'Go and tell Raza Miyan that Sharda's mother has come to see him. Ask him to come right away.'

Raza and Munnu arrived within ten minutes.

Devi spoke with tearful eyes, 'After you both went away, I had to leave my house. Your visit to my place last night has wreaked havoc in my life. I'll tell you later what has happened. Please arrange for a house for me. It should be such that Babu Sahib cannot find it. Else he won't leave me alive.'

Raza looked at Munnu as if to let him know how good their plan was. He said to Devi, 'Don't you worry at all, I'll find you a house which even Babu Sahib's father will not be able to find! You need not bother. We will shed our blood for your sweat. To tell you the truth, Madam, Babu Sahib never really deserved you.'

Munnu echoed the words of his partner-in-crime, 'You said it, brother. You are fit to be a queen. I used to tell you, Madam, that Babuji has a habit of going to Dalmandi, but you never believed me. I saw him stepping out of Gulabjaan's terrace last night. He was heavily drunk.'

Devi hissed, 'That's a lie! He has no such habit. He has a bad temper and loses his senses in a fury but he is not a bad person.'

Munnu tried coaxing her, 'Madam, why don't you believe me? All right, if I show you someday, then will you believe me?'

Raza interrupted him quickly, 'Show her later, right now you take her to my place. Take her upstairs. I'll go and arrange for a house in the meantime. It's going to be perfect for you.'

Devi asked, 'There must be a lot of women in your house?'

Raza replied courteously, 'There is nobody, Madam, except an old aunt. She will arrange for a water-bearer for you. I'll go and look for a house.'

Devi pleaded, 'Take a look at my place too, see if Babu Sahib is back home.'

Raza said, 'I am annoyed with Babu Sahib now. I might just pick up a fight with him if I see him. A man who cannot respect a beauty like you is not a man.'

Munnu agreed, 'You're absolutely right, brother. I don't understand how he can rebuke an innocent woman like her! I've been serving Madam for years, but she has never raised her voice at me.'

Raza left in search of a house and the tonga proceeded towards Raza's house.

Suddenly, Devi started harbouring doubts. *Are these two truly rogues? But how to find out?* It was true that Devi had abandoned her husband for a better life, but in that short span of time she had begun to regret this decision! How would she live alone in a house? What would she do alone? She wasn't able to really make up her mind. She felt in her heart, *Why not go back home? God willing, he may not have come back yet.* She said to Munnu, 'You run along and see if Babuji has returned.'

'You go and rest, I'll go and find out,' encouraged Munnu.

Devi stood stiff, 'I will not go inside.'

'I swear to God, the whole house is empty. You doubt us! We are one of those who, at your command, can jump into fire,' Munnu cajoled her.

Devi alighted from the tonga and went inside. The bird, now caught, flapped its wings, but could not gain its flight because its feet were stuck with birdlime, and the huntsman kept it in his bag. Will that helpless creature ever be able to fly again? Will she able to sit and chirp on the branches again?

When Shyamkishore returned home in the morning, his state of mind was peaceful. He was doubtful whether Devi would be at home. When he saw the door ajar, his heart stopped beating for a second. Open doors in the morning were not a good sign. He stood at the door for a moment and looked inside. He couldn't hear a sound. He went to the courtyard; it had been left abandoned. Upstairs too, all was silent! The sight of an empty house was gnawing at him! Shyamkishore now started looking around a bit cautiously. There was no money in the trunk. The jewellery box was also empty. No doubt was left in his mind. When someone goes to take a dip in the holy Ganga, they don't take all the money with them. She had left for good. Now there was no doubt whatsoever. He also knew where she had gone. Perhaps she could be brought back this instant, but what would the world say? Shyamkishore sat down on the bed and started pondering over the matter calmly. He was sure that it was Raza and Munnu who had instigated her. After all, what else could Babuji have done? He left the old house, and constantly tried to explain things to Devi. What else could he have done? Was it wrong to have hit her? Even if it were to be deemed wrong for a second, was it right of Devi to have left the house in this manner? Had there been another woman who didn't have venom injected in her heart already, would she have left the house after being hit by her husband? Certainly, Devi's heart was blemished now.

Babu Sahib thought again, *The maid will come any minute. If she doesn't find her in the house, what will she think? The news will spread like fire in the colony. Oh God, what do I do?*

There was no regret or kindness in Shyamkishore's heart at the moment. If he could find Devi somehow, he wouldn't hesitate to kill her on the spot. Her decision to leave the house, even if in a state of frenzy, was unforgivable in his eyes. Anger can often lead to insensitivity. He began to hate the world. When one's own wife can cheat, then what is to be expected from others? The woman for whom he would live and die, for whom he was ready to compromise all at any minute—when she could not be his, then what could one expect from others? What had he not done to keep this woman happy? He had fought with his own family, severed ties with his brothers, so much so that they didn't even want to see his face any more. There was not a single wish of hers which he did not fulfil. Whenever she had even a minor headache, he would get worried. He used to look after her throughout the night. The same woman had betrayed him today, that too after believing that rogue. She had sullied his face. But accusing that rogue was like consoling his own heart. How can someone be easily influenced if the heart is pure and clear? He thought, *If this woman has betrayed me, then there is no such thing as love and trust in this world. These emotions are merely a figment of the imagination of a few emotional creatures. Apart from sadness and hopelessness, there is nothing to imbibe from this world. All right, you wicked woman. You're a free spirit from now on; you can do what you want. Now there is no one to hold your hand. You have done this cruel injustice to the person whom you always called your 'beloved', you have been so insincere to him! I can drag you to court to get you punished, but then what's the use! God himself will punish you for your deeds.*

Shyamkishore went down the stairs quietly. He didn't say anything to anyone nor did he hear from anybody. Leaving the door unlatched, he walked towards the banks of the Ganga.

Translated from the Hindi by Shirin Bismillah

Godavari's Suicide

1

Pandit Devdutt had been married a long time but had no children. As long as his parents were alive, they continued to pester him to remarry but he didn't agree. He loved his wife, Godavari, deeply. He did not want to put an end to his marital bliss in the quest for progeny. Moreover, he was an enlightened man with a clear sense of responsibility towards children. He believed that a man should only marry as long as he was competent enough to bring up his children and educate them well. Earlier, when he saw children laughing and playing, he felt a stab in his heart. But now, like many of his compatriots, he suffered from various physical ailments. The thought of children now frightened him.

However, Godavari was not one to give up so easily. To begin with, she relied on gods and deities, charms and amulets, chants and incantations. But when she saw that none of these were proving fruitful, she planned to get her husband, Panditji, married again. She spent weeks and months thinking over this. She tried to drive the thought away from her mind but it had taken a firm hold on her and refused to go away.

She knew that it required a great sacrifice on her part. She might even lose her husband's love. She wondered if it were ever possible. Couldn't the tree of love she had tended for fifteen long years withstand the buffet of a storm? Eventually Godavari submitted to her fervent longing for a child and got ready to welcome a *saut*, a co-wife, in her life.

2

Pandit Devdutt broke into laughter when he heard Godavari's proposal. He surmised that she was either testing his love or wanting to gauge his true feelings. He dismissed the suggestion out of hand. But Godavari was dead serious about her plan. 'Don't treat this lightly. I'm telling you the truth. To have a child in the house, I'm ready to put up with the ignominy of living with your second wife.' Her eyes filled with tears as she said this. Devdutt realized that Godavari was indeed serious about her plan. He hugged Godavari warmly for this demonstration of her selflessness but said, 'I can't do this. I have no desire for any offspring.'

'You may not, but I do. You must do it for me, if not for yourself,' Godavari persisted.

Panditji was a simple man. He did not quite agree to the proposal, but was persuaded to acquiesce to it. That was enough for Godavari. Panditji had to take no initiative, Godavari's efforts made things easy for him. She not only used her own money for the wedding expenses, but gave away her clothes and jewellery to the saut as well. What Panditji feared the most was public ridicule. He wondered with trepidation what people would say when they saw him bereft of his moustache and wearing the bridegroom's crown.

'The colleagues in my office will make fun of me, smiling meaningfully at each other. Their piercing gaze will be sharper than knives. Where will I hide my face then?'

Godavari went to her village, set herself the task of implementing her plan and brought it to a satisfactory end. The new bride came home. Godavari was happy as though she had brought home a bride for her son. She joined in the dancing and singing. Little did she know that very soon her singing would turn to lamentations.

3

Several months passed. Godavari ordered her saut about like a mother-in-law, even though she didn't forget for a moment that she wasn't. On the other hand, Gomti was fully conscious of her status in the household. Even though Godavari was not as domineering as a real mother-in-law might have been, Gomti resented the way Godavari threw her weight around. She felt embarrassed when she had to beg Godavari for every little necessity of daily life.

After some days, a distinct change was seen in Godavari's demeanour. She began to keep a close watch on Panditji's movements when he went out or returned. Her normal calmness disappeared and she began to find fault with every little thing. As soon as Panditji returned home from office, Godavari perched herself beside him and began a long litany of complaints against Gomti. By the time she finished her litany, Panditji felt as if a great weight had been laid on his chest. It was difficult to understand why Godavari had become so communicative. Probably, she felt insecure about Gomti, about her beauty and her bashful eyes. Having broken the dam, she was attempting to stop the deluge of water with a few clods of earth.

One day, Godavari asked Gomti to prepare sweet rice that needed milk, rice and sugar. Perhaps it was the festival of Raksha Bandhan. Gomti replied, 'There's no sugar in the house.'

Godavari was stunned to hear this. 'How could so much sugar disappear so soon? Only the person who breaks his back to earn money knows how it is. How could those who only sit at home and consume know?'

When Panditji returned home from work, this little incident reached his ears in an exaggerated version of domestic indiscretion. For a while, Panditji wondered if Gomti suffered from some kind of chronic hunger.

A similar incident occurred a few days later. Panditji suffered from piles. He did not eat red chillies. Earlier, when Godavari cooked, she took special care of this fact. One day, Gomti added a pinch of red chilli to the spices in the lentils. Panditji ate very little of it. But Godavari made Gomti's life miserable for this. 'Such a tongue should be burnt!' she said viciously.

4

Panditji was a simple man. He returned home from office, ate his meal and then went to sleep. He subscribed to a weekly paper. It would often remain unread for months. He went to great lengths to avoid doing anything that required the slightest exertion or discomfort. Sometimes he received passes for the theatre from his office but he never used them. Others borrowed his passes and went instead. Probably Panditji had never gone

to a Ramlila performance in his entire office life. Godavari
had understood his nature very well. Panditji also found it
convenient to abide by Godavari's advice in every matter.

But even soft cotton, constantly pressed, turns hard.
Panditji found this constant nagging intolerable and felt
annoyed. His will power, which had remained dormant all
these years, began to surface slowly.

He acknowledged that Godavari had made a great sacrifice
by bringing home Gomti. It could even be called beyond
human proclivities. But he thought, if she had done any
favour, it was to him. 'It's no favour to Gomti. Why should she
be treated with such insensitivity? What great happiness did
Gomti find here that she should put up with such rudeness?
She had a husband who was an old man and chronically ill. She
had a home, but there was no guarantee for meals if the master
lost his job.' In these circumstances, Godavari's oppressive
behaviour seemed highly disagreeable to Panditji.

Godavari had enough prescience to understand Devdutt's
feelings. She could clearly gauge what was going through his
mind by looking at his face. If this made her jealous of Gomti,
it also made her resentful of Pandit Devdutt's selfishness,
disloyalty and betrayal. As a result, the bitterness kept rising.

5

Gradually, Godavari stopped talking about Gomti with
Panditji. It was almost as if Gomti did not exist in the house.
She did not care whether Gomti had eaten or not, whether
she needed new clothes or any other things. Once, for several
days, Gomti was not given any snacks at teatime. Panditji

noticed this meanness but, because he was laid-back by
nature and did not want to create disturbance in his peaceful
existence, he chose to remain silent. However, this last act of
cruelty was too much even for him to bear. One day, he asked
Godavari with some trepidation, 'Don't you buy sweetmeats
for tea any more?'

Godavari was incensed. 'If you don't bring them, from
where will they come? Do I have a servant here to run errands
for me?'

Godavari's words pierced Devdutt's heart like an arrow.
She had never spoken to him like this before.

'Speak softly. I haven't said anything to get so flustered.'

Godavari lowered her gaze and replied, 'I speak in the
way that I'm accustomed to. I can't speak glibly like some
other people.'

Devdutt's anger flared. 'I just don't understand your
moods these days. You start squabbling over every little thing.'

Godavari's face turned red with anger. She had been
sitting all this while, now she stood up. Her lips quivered.
'Now you won't like anything about me. I'm full of blemishes
from head to toe. There are others now who can carry out
your wishes. I can't do it any more. Here, take the keys to
your tin trunk. You must take care of your money and wealth
yourself. Enough of these daily squabbles. I've put up with it
this far but can't do it any more.'

Pandit Devdutt got a rude shock. The pettiness of domestic
squabbles, which he always feared, now entered his house in
a dreadful form. He did not say anything as it would only
have made matters worse. He went out wondering whether he
had wronged Godavari in any way that she was behaving so
strangely. He had no idea how the house would be managed

if Godavari refused to run it. She had always managed to run it on such a meagre income. 'Now only God can help us. She must be placated, there's simply no other option. After all, what can Gomti do? The responsibility will fall on me. Godavari might come around, but it's not going to be easy.'

Panditji's hopes proved futile. For three days, the keys lay right there in the courtyard like a poisonous cobra. Nobody dared go anywhere near them. On the fourth day, Panditji mustered up the courage to pick it up. At that moment he felt as though someone had placed a mountain on his head. Indolent people find it very difficult to shift even an inch from their appointed path.

Although Panditji knew well that he would not be able to run the house due to work in his office, he did not have the audacity to hand the keys over to Gomti. But this was a mere pretence. Gomti had to do all the chores even though the keys stayed with him. Thus, the responsibility of running the household was finally out of Godavari's hands. Along with the keys, the status of the mistress of the house also slipped away from her. Within no time, the change in the attitudes of the maid and the neighbourhood women towards her became apparent. Godavari was now the dethroned queen. Now she only evoked people's sympathy, nothing more.

6

With this shift in the management of the household, a regrettable change took place in Godavari. Jealousy is a sentiment that cannot be suppressed for long. The neighbours discussed the goings-on in this household all day. 'See, how selfish this world is! The poor woman shot herself in the foot by getting her husband remarried. She even gave away her clothes and jewellery. Now, she's crying bitter tears. Well, a saut will always be a saut, but now even her husband has turned against her. All she can do now is to stay in the house like a maid and suffer. Is this life worth living?'

Such words of sympathy only served to inflame Godavari's jealousy. She didn't realize that false sympathy like this generally stemmed from the human tendency to take perverse pleasure in the suffering of others.

However, the situation of which Godavari was sure and Panditji feared, did not take place. No problem was encountered in the running of the household. Yes, due to a lack of experience, Panditji's management was somewhat less efficient than Godavari's, which resulted in a lot more expense but the house was running quite well. Of course, Godavari found Gomti's household skills quite clumsy. Jealousy is a fire that lacks the attribute of expansiveness. It doesn't expand our generosity, it contracts it. Now, if the household suffered any losses, it made Godavari happy rather than sad.

It was the rainy season. The sun could not be seen in the sky for several days. Clothes in trunks grew mildewed and the sesame pickle went bad. Gomti didn't take care to put them out in the sun. Godavari observed these losses but felt no regret. On the contrary, it gave her the opportunity to make some caustic remarks about Gomti's clumsiness as a housewife.

There was a change in Pandit Devdutt's behaviour too. As long as Godavari had managed the house competently, he was perfectly satisfied with her arrangement. He was not even required to go to the market to buy vegetables. Now Godavari could see him running to the market several times a day. As the household was not run on a planned schedule, he would be seen rushing to the bazaar at odd hours. Godavari observed all this and commented loudly so that everyone could hear, 'This is the same maharaja who wouldn't lift a straw earlier. Now it seems he keeps rushing to the market the entire a day. It doesn't interfere with his studies!'

Godavari had found out long ago that Panditji was not very good at getting a good bargain while shopping. Whenever she needed clothes, she would get them through Lala Sahib, an elderly neighbour. Panditji had all but forgotten that Godavari, too, needed saris once in a while. As long as someone else did what was, in fact, his responsibility, it suited his temperament. He would gladly wear what Godavari got for him. He didn't care at all for new fashions and designs. But now he had to go the bazaar to even buy clothes.

Once it so happened that Gomti needed a few saris. Panditji went to the market and bought some nice ones for her. The haberdasher charged him a high price. Panditji had no qualms in buying on credit. Gomti showed the new clothes to Godavari. Turning her face away, Godavari said, 'At least you've taught him that he should buy clothes for his family. I've spent sixteen years with him without ever having the good luck to wear anything bought by him.'

Incidents such as these further aggravated Godavari's jealousy of Gomti. As long as she had believed that Panditji was dull by nature, she didn't have any complaint. But now, when she saw all these changes in him, she felt that Panditji's love, which had eluded her despite all her efforts, had now been won over by Gomti because of her youth. What Godavari had so far perceived as his love in fact, all pretence, born out of self-interest.

7

It so happened that Gomti fell ill. She didn't have even the strength to move about. Godavari had to take on the responsibility of cooking. She suspected that Gomti was not really sick. It was a mean ploy to make her do the cooking. She grumbled to the neighbours, 'They wanted to make a maidservant of me and now their wishes are fulfilled.'

During mealtimes, Panditji seemed to be in haste. For some reason, he was scared to be alone with Godavari, lest she begin her litany of grievances. While eating, he dreaded this prospect the most. Godavari observed this with her sharp eyes and felt offended. One day, she couldn't take it anymore. She said, 'Have you been asked not to talk to me? You can go on talking with others the entire night but it seems you've taken a vow not to open your mouth in my presence. You can see how the household is being run, can't you? Everything's happening the way you want it.'

Panditji lowered his head and said, 'Hmm, it runs the way it's being run. I can't worry myself to death about it, can I? If you're bent upon destroying this house, what can I do about it?'

Hearing this, Godavari exchanged some harsh words. Things became worse. Panditji stood up in a huff, leaving his meal. Godavari coaxed him to sit down again, but he was not to be persuaded! Then she closed the kitchen and everyone had to fast that day.

There was something special about Gomti—she could put up with the harshest of words but could not bear hunger. That's why she never fasted although, due to peer pressure, she did fast on *Janmashtami*. But, lately, since her illness, she felt even hungrier. When she saw that it was past noon and there was no sign of a meal being cooked, she grew desperate and sent for some sweetmeats from the bazaar. It's quite possible that this was done only to tease Godavari because, after all, people do not die if they miss a meal. Godavari fumed within. Immediately, she also sent for some sweetmeats. After many years, she ate them to her heart's content. Such are the miracles wrought by envy!

The same Godavari, who considered it a sin to touch even a drop of water before noon, now discovered that she could not stay without eating breakfast early in the morning. Earlier, she always used sesame oil to massage her head. Now she found it gave her a headache. She also developed the habit of chewing paan. Envy made her behave like a newly wedded bride.

The auspicious day of Janmashtami arrived. For these two days, Panditji's habitual passivity would always disappear. He made preparations with great enthusiasm. Godavari was very particular about the fast on this occasion, not eating any snacks or even drinking a drop of water. As for Panditji, he was a great devotee of Lord Krishna. This time, at his instance, Gomti also mustered the courage to observe the fast. However, she was greatly surprised when the maid informed her that Godavari was not fasting and had asked for some puris to be brought from the market.

In the evening, Godavari intended to go to the temple and asked for an ekka to be ordered. Gomti found this demand unreasonable. For one thing, the temple was quite near and then the ekka drivers always acted pricey on this day and charged higher fares. She said haughtily, 'We have no money to waste. The temple isn't all that far away. Let her go on foot. It's easy to make demands, the one who has to earn the money knows how difficult it is.' Three years ago, Gomti had had to listen to Godavari saying exactly the same words. Now, Gomti was paying her back in the same coin. How time changes things!

Godavari became more careless while cooking meals. She was no longer concerned, as earlier, about the kind of food that agreed with Panditji's system. One day, she asked the maid to take out the spices on her own and grind them. When daal was cooked with the same spices, they turned out to be too hot. Panditji was too scared to complete his meal. Like other indolent people he, too, was fond of spicy food, but he had to exercise restraint because of his ailment. When Gomti heard of this she raised her eyebrows and said, 'Has old age loosened his tongue?'

Once Godavari had made a similar jibe, but now it was her turn to listen to it. Oh, the vicissitudes of life!

8

Godavari decided to embrace the Ganga. Three years ago, she had gone with the newlyweds, her husband and Gomti, to offer flowers and milk to the sacred river. Now, she had come to offer her life to it, wanting to rest forever in its joyful waves.

Every moment in that house had become a painful experience for Godavari. It was impossible for a self-respecting woman like her to live as a maid in the same house where she had once been the queen! Her bond with that house had become like an old rope—constantly breaking at the points where the knots were tied. She could think of no other option other than seeking refuge in the Ganga.

For several days, Godavari had been threatening to kill herself. This annoyed Panditji who said nonchalantly, 'I wish you would die!'

Godavari still remembered those poisonous words. She never forgot the hurtful words people said to her. Gomti, too, had repeated those words today, even though she said them under grave provocation. However, Godavari had forgotten what harsh words she herself had spoken. Only Gomti's words echoed in her ears. And Panditji had not even reprimanded her for saying such things. 'Such injustice was done to me,' she thought, 'and he did not even utter a word in my favour!'

That night, after everyone had retired, Godavari left home. Dark clouds overcast the sky. The rain was falling in sheets. Tears streamed down Godavari's face. The bond of love was so strong and, at the same time, so fragile! Fragile in the face of betrayal and strong at the prospect of separation! Godavari stood at the doorstep and wept for hours, remembering so many things from the past. Once she had received love, honour and the comforts of life in that house. But all of these were things of the past. Presently, she remembered Panditji's cruel words and tears began to flow from her eyes. The next moment, Godavari set off from the house.

If, at that moment, Pandit Devdutt had run after her, drenched in the rain, bareheaded and barefooted, held her in a tight embrace and uttered the word, 'Beloved!' and nothing more, could Godavari have remained steadfast in her resolve?

It was the month of Kunwar in the autumn season. The waves in the river roared threateningly at night. Whenever there was a flash of lightning, the leaping waves appeared to be like so many mad elephants splashing about in the water. A fearsome vision of the struggle of life spread before her eyes.

Godavari's heart was also experiencing a tumult of emotions that collided with each other and then disappeared. Where did they go, she wondered. 'Into the darkness, where there's nothing.' Could that roaring, gushing river set Godavari's restless heart at rest? The waves did not convey the sound of harmony, nor did they have any compassion. At that moment, they had a terrifying and fearsome aspect.

Godavari was sitting on the riverbank, thinking. Who could say what were her thoughts? Was she still hoping that Pandit Devdutt might turn up at any moment. The bond of love was ever so strong.

The luckless woman, torn between jealousy, despair and life's cruelty, fell into the lap of the Ganga. The waves enveloped her from all sides and the mighty river swallowed her.

Dawn broke. Godavari was not to be found in the house. There was a letter lying on her charpai that read—

Swami,

I did not have anyone else in the world except you. I gave all I had to make you happy. Now, your happiness demands that I should leave this world. Therefore, I offer you my life. Please forgive the wrongs I have committed. May God always keep you happy!

As Panditji read the letter, he fell down unconscious. Gomti began to cry. But it was not clear why.

Translated from the Urdu by M. Asaduddin

The Co-wife

1

After Razia had two to three children who died and she had lost her youth, Ramu's love for her started diminishing. The desire for a second marriage occupied his thoughts.

He started bickering with Razia every day. He would find one or the other excuse to lose his temper and beat Razia. And then, finally, he got home a new wife. Her name was Dasi or Dasia. She was youthful, big-eyed and as fair as the *champa* flower. How could the pale and feeble Razia compete with this girl! Even so, she tried to retain her authority and maintain her slackening hold over the household for as long as she could. But this was like trying to prevent a crumbling roof from falling with inadequate support. She had painstakingly built this house. She could not bear to leave it so easily. And she was not so stupid that she would leave the house and go, thereby allowing Dasi to rule over it.

2

One day, Razia told Ramu, 'I don't have saris; go and get one for me.'

Only a day before Ramu had got a Chanderi sari for Dasi. Hearing Razia's demand he said, 'I don't have money now.'

Razia did not crave much for saris; what she really wanted was to put obstacles in the way of Ramu and Dasi's happiness. She said, 'If you did not have money, why did you buy the Chanderi for your darling? In place of that, you could have bought two saris with the same money; then I could have used one.'

Expressing his independence, Ramu said, 'It's my will. I will do what I want. Who are you to question me? She's young, it's time for her to have fun and enjoy herself. You want her to be engrossed in the worries of the household right now? I can't do this. If you want to wear fineries then go and work. Hasn't God given you hands and feet? Earlier, you used to wake up at the crack of dawn and start working. Now, you keep gloating in spite and malice against her the entire day. Will money fall from the skies? Why should I give up my life for you?'

Razia asked, 'Am I her maid that I should do all the work in the house while she sits like a queen? All these days I have worked really hard and this is the result I get. I am not going to take it any more.'

'You will have to stay the way I keep you.'

'I will stay if I want to, or I will live separately.'

'Do what you want but get off my back.'

'Well said. From today, I relieve you. I will think that I'm a widow now.'

3

Ramu knew that the household was put together by Razia, even though she lacked beauty that pleased the eye. It was quite possible that he would have made up with Razia after a while, but Dasi too was no less cunning. She decided to strike while the iron was hot. She said, 'What got madam angry today?'

Ramu replied with an air of carelessness, 'It was because of your Chanderi that Razia raised hell. Now she says that she will stay separately. I have told her to do what she wants.'

Rolling her eyes, Dasi said, 'These are all tantrums to make one plead with her, to beg before her. You sit quietly. In a day or two, she will cool down. You don't say anything; if you do then her temper will shoot sky-high!'

Ramu said in a serious tone, 'Dasi, you have no idea how proud she is. Once she says something, she does it.'

Razia did not expect Ramu to be so thankless. She wasn't as beautiful as she once was, which is why Ramu did not love her any more. This was not an unusual thing for a man to do; but Ramu separating from her was something she couldn't believe. This house had been put together bit by bit with the money she had saved. The household too had been put together by her. It was she who had started selling vegetables. She had to face great hardship after coming to this house. And for what? Only to eat a coarse meal and retire into a corner after a weary day! Today she was thrown out of the house with such unkindness, as if she was a fly in the milk! Ramu didn't even say this much: 'You cannot stay separately. Either I will die here or I will kill you, but I will not let you live separately. You are married to me. This is no trivial matter.'

When Ramu did not care for her, why should she worry about him? Do all men with wives keep sitting, doing no work? Everyone else has their mothers or fathers, sons or grandsons. Had his sons been alive, would he have dared to bring in a new wife? Would I be so distressed then? What a heartless fellow that he did not have even a trace of mercy for me!

The woman in her rebelled against such torture owing to her situation of dependence. The same fire that cannot light a log of wood can set a flower aflame!

4

The very next day, Razia left for another village. She took nothing with her. The sari draped across her body was all that she owned. God had already snatched her sons from her. Today, He took away her house.

When she left, Ramu was so engrossed with his young wife that he hardly noticed that Razia was leaving for good. At least that is what Razia thought. She did not want to leave like a thief. She wanted to show Dasi and her husband and the entire village that she was not taking a thing from the house. Her objective was to humiliate Ramu before the village. If she left quietly none of this would happen. Instead, Ramu would claim that Razia had taken away everything from the house.

She called out to Ramu and said, 'Now look after your house. I am going. I am not taking a thing from your house.'

For a moment, Ramu was rendered speechless. He could not fathom what to say. He did not think that she would go like this. He had expected her to try and take everything from the house and seek the sympathy of the villagers. What to do now?

Dasi said, 'Go and blow your trumpet in the village. Here nobody fears anything. What did you get from your house when you came here that gives you the right to take away something?'

Instead of bickering with her, Razia said to Ramu, 'Do you hear what your darling says? I will still not open my mouth. I am going but, Dassorani, you too will not rule for long like a queen. In the divine court of the Lord, wrongdoings don't bear fruit. The haughtiness of many a man has been broken to bits by Him.'

Dasi laughed but Ramu lowered his head. Razia went away.

5

The new village that Razia went to shared borders with Ramu's village. The people there knew her. They knew how skilled a housewife she was, how hard-working and how honest she was. She faced no obstacles in getting work there. The one who works double compared to others on the same wage is hardly deprived of employment.

If one starts describing how Razia spent three long years, how she built another household and how she started farming, then one could write a book. She knew the secrets of saving well. She gained confidence and did not need any male patronage to survive on her own. Seeing her work tirelessly, the villagers thought that she was trying to show Ramu that 'I can live without you in comfort'.

Razia was no longer a dependent woman. She lived off her earnings.

She had a pair of sturdy bulls. She did not merely give them fodder; she also fed them two rotis every day and would stroke them for hours. Sometimes she would place her head on their shoulder and weep, saying, 'And I tell you, you two are all that I have—you are my sons as well as my husband. My honour is in your hands now.'

The bulls probably understood Razia's language and emotions, but they were not human beings. Lowering their heads, they would keep licking Razia's hands to console her. When they saw her, they would look at her with a lot of fondness in their eyes; they would swing their shoulders happily, allowing her to yoke them together, and would work very hard for her. Those who have looked after bulls and loved them wholeheartedly can alone understand this.

Razia was the chaudhurain of the village now. Earlier her mind was always searching for an anchor and she could not develop freely. But now, as she came out of the shadow, she improved and matured.

One day, after Razia returned home, a man told her, 'Did you not hear, chaudhurain, that Ramu is very ill? I heard that he has been unable to eat for ten days.'

Razia said with an air of indifference, 'Is it an ague?'

'No, it is not an ague. It is some other disease. He was lying on a cot outside the house. I asked, "How are you, Ramuji?" and he started crying. He is in bad shape. There is not a penny in the house for him to get medicines. Dasi has a son now. She never tried working before, and now that she has a child how can she go to work? All the blame is on Ramu's head. And she keeps demanding ornaments and clothes—she is still a new bride!'

Stepping into her house, Razia said, 'One has to suffer for one's actions.'

But she didn't feel at ease inside. She was out in a moment. Probably she wanted to ask the man something in a way that would not reveal her concern.

But the man had left. Razia looked for him everywhere, but he was not to be found. She sat on the threshold and remembered her words from three years ago when she had decided to leave Ramu's house. At that time, she had cursed him out of jealousy. Now, there was no heartburn. Time had calmed her down. The miserable plight of Ramu and Dasi did not evoke envy any more; they deserved mercy.

She thought that if Ramu had not been able to eat anything for ten days, then certainly his situation was not good. He had never been very stout or healthy; these ten days of fasting must have weakened him further. The farms too must have been neglected. He may not have got adequate food either . . .

A woman from the neighbourhood, who came on the pretext of borrowing fire, asked, 'Heard that Ramu is very sick. You get what you deserve. One would not turn out one's enemy as cruelly as he turned you out of his house.'

Razia cut in, 'No, sister, it was not like that. The poor man had said nothing. Whatever he did was because he was being controlled by Dasi; he never said anything to me on his own. Why should I speak ill of anyone? Which man does not come under the spell of women? Dasi is responsible for the state he is in.'

The neighbour went away without borrowing the fire she had come for. Instead, she turned her face away and left.

Razia picked up an earthen pot and the line to draw water from the well. It was time to feed and water the bulls, but her eyes were fixed on the road that led to Malsa, Ramu's village. Certainly someone would come to call her. After all, how could she visit him without being asked to? People would say, 'See! Didn't she finally come back running?'

But Ramu must be unconscious. Being without food for ten days is not a small matter. What must his body be left with? And then, who would call her? What interest did Dasi have to do so? She could start another family. There would be hundred clients ready. Oh yes, there is someone coming. Yes, someone is coming. He looks like a disturbed soul. Who is this man? I never saw him in Malsa, but then I have not been there for so long. Some new people must have settled down there.

Suddenly a man appeared beside the well. He was possibly a wayfarer. Razia kept the pot down and advanced towards the stranger. She asked, 'Has Ramu Mahto sent you? All right, come home But I will take some time. I have to feed and water the bulls and light the evening lamp. I will give you money; go and give it to Dasi. Tell her to send word if she needs anything.'

What did this footslogger know of Ramu? He belonged to another village. First, he was surprised, but then he understood. Quietly, he went with Razia.

On the way, Razia asked him, 'And what is his condition like now?'

The wayfarer speculated and said, 'He is slightly better.'

'I hope Dasi is not crying too much?'

'She didn't cry.'

'Why should she cry? She would understand later.'

After the traveller went away after taking the money, Razia fed the bulls. But her mind was preoccupied with Ramu. Fond memories resurfaced like little starlets in her mind. She remembered the time she had fallen ill. It was ten years ago. How he had sat beside her all through the day and night. He had even forgotten to eat and drink. It came to her mind then, why not go and see him? Who will say what? Who would dare to say anything? I am not going to steal. I am going to the man I stayed with for fifteen to twenty years. Dasi would wrinkle up her nose. Let her do so. What do I have to do with her?

Razia latched the door and left the house in the care of a worker. She set off to see Ramu, trembling and hesitating, with the gift of forgiveness.

6

Ramu realized within a few days that the soul of his household had left. He knew that no matter how hard he tried, he could not get his energy back. Dasi was pretty and fashionable, but snobbish. When the first phase of passion died down, the bickering began. The farms started yielding less and whatever there was got squandered away in sundry expenses. Loans had to be taken. It was this worry and sorrow that affected his health. In the beginning, he did not bother much. What could he do by bothering? There was no money in the house. The treatment by quacks led to the disease becoming deep-rooted. Now for ten to twelve days he had been unable to eat or drink. He lay moaning on his cot, waiting for death.

His situation was such that he was certain about his future, so he rested in thoughts of the past like a vehicle that goes into reverse on finding the road ahead blocked. He kept crying, remembering Razia and cursing Dasi, saying, 'It is because of you alone that I turned her out of the house. With her departure, Goddess Lakshmi too went away. I know that if I call her even now, she would come running, but what face do I have to call her? If she comes just once and I can seek her forgiveness, I will die happy. I have no other desire.'

Just then Razia came in. Placing her palm on his forehead, she asked, 'How is your health? I came to know about your condition today.'

Ramu looked at her with tearful eyes but could not say anything. He folded his hands to greet her. And that was when his eyes rolled up and his hands remained folded.

7

The corpse was in the house. Razia was weeping but Dasi was worried. There was no money in the house. Wood was needed for the pyre and arrangements had to be made for refreshments for at least those who would shoulder the corpse. And how could the body be taken away without a shroud? It would cost at least ten rupees. But there were not even ten paise in the house. She was scared that she would have to sacrifice her jewellery. The ornaments weren't even that precious! After all, what capacity did a farmer have? One could perhaps get ten rupees by selling one or two pieces. What else could be done? She called the headman's son and said, '*Devarji*, how do I cross this hurdle? There is not a soul in the village who would place a jot of trust in me. I have some ornaments. Tell the headman to keep them as security so that we can tide over the crisis today; after that God is our keeper!'

'Why don't you ask Razia?'

All at once, Razia came from within, wiping her eyes. Their exchange wafted into her ears. She asked, 'What is it?

What are you discussing? Is this the time to talk; shouldn't you take the body for cremation?'

'Yes, of course, that is what we are arranging for.'

'There wouldn't be any money here. Everything must have been spent to treat his illness. He has left this wretched one midstream. You run to the other house, Brother. How far is it after all. Take the keys. Tell the worker there to take out fifty rupees from the store. Tell him that it is kept on the top of the stave.'

When he left, Dasi fell to her knees weeping, holding Razia's feet. Razia's sisterly words touched her. She saw how kind and forgiving Razia was.

Razia embraced her and said, 'Why do you cry, Sister? He has gone, but I am still here. Don't worry about anything. In this very house, both you and I will live in his name. I will look after here as well as there. It is only half a mile away. If anybody asks for your ornaments, don't give them.'

Dasi felt like banging her head and killing herself. How she had tortured Razia and made her cry, and how she had rested only after turning her out of the house!

Razia asked, 'Make a list of those whom you owe money to and tell me. I don't want to maintain any quarrel. Why is the child looking so weak?'

Dasia said, 'I have no milk in me. The cow you had left behind died. The child does not get milk.'

'Oh God! The poor thing has wilted! Tomorrow I will get a cow. I will get the entire household here. What is there to hold me back?'

The corpse was taken for cremation amidst a lot of bustle. Razia went with it. She conducted the last rites. There was feasting. It all came to some two hundred rupees. There was no need to borrow any money.

The precious qualities in Dasi too were revealed during this crisis, in this burning flame of sacrifice. The pretty coquette had turned into an icon of service.

8

Today, it has been seven years since Ramu's death. Razia is looking after the house. She does not consider Dasi to be her co-wife; she considers her a daughter. She ensures Dasi has enough clothes before buying any for her own use. She ensures Dasi eats before she does. Jokhu goes to study now. His engagement is almost final. In their caste, marriages are fixed during childhood.

Dasi said, 'Sister, what is the need to get ornaments made? My jewellery is all intact.'

Razia replied, 'No, dear! I will make new ornaments for her. I can still work. When I am tired, do what you want. You are still in the age to wear fine things; you keep your ornaments.'

Nayin Thakur wistfully said, 'Had Jokhu's father been here today, things would have been different.'

Razia said, 'He is not here, but I am. I will do double of what he would have done. When I die, then say Jokhu's father is no more.'

On the day of the wedding, seeing Dasi weep, Razia said, 'Bahu, why do you cry? I am still alive. This house is yours. You live as you like. Give me some morsels to eat, that's it. What else can I do? My husband has died. But yours is still alive.'

Dasi placed her head on Razia's lap and cried her heart out. 'Sister, you are like my mother. If you were not here, whose door would I be standing at? Rats would have returned to the house. In his tenure, I had to suffer a lot. The happiness of married life, I enjoyed during your tenure. I am not crying out of sadness; I am crying over God's kindness towards a hapless one like me; where am I and where is this prosperity!'

Razia smiled as tears rolled down her eyes.

Translated from the Hindi by Anuradha Ghosh

Two Sisters

1

The two sisters met after two years in a relative's house.

After weeping with excitement, the elder one, Rupkumari, noticed that her younger sister, Ramdulari, was adorned in ornaments from head to toe. Her complexion looked more radiant, her behaviour more dignified and she sounded cleverer in her conversations now. A costly Benaresi sari and a jujube-red, embroidered velvet blouse had further added to her beauty. Rupkumari wondered whether she was the same Ramdulari, who looked so unkempt in her childhood and would boisterously play around with her dishevelled hair. Rupkumari had last seen her two years ago, on the day of her wedding. Even then, there had been no significant change in her appearance. Although she had grown taller, but she was as lean, idiotic and muddle-headed as ever. She would get upset at petty things. But today, she looked different, radiant—as though a flower had blossomed. Where had she concealed this beauty all this time? No, maybe it was just illusory—not genuine beauty, but rather the power of attracting others' gaze through one's dress and ornaments. Merely wearing silk, velvet and gold ornaments cannot make one beautiful. Still, it pleased the eyes. Many women had gathered there, but none of them could exude such an attractive and magical appeal.

If a mirror were nearby, Rupkumari would have certainly appraised herself in it. No doubt, she had seen herself in the mirror just before leaving home and tried her best to beautify herself as much as she could. But now, unable to conjure a clear image of her own embellished face, she was becoming impatient to catch a glimpse of herself again. Now, she would compare her beauty with Ramdulari's and try to unravel the mystery behind the latter's allure. Though she carried a small mirror in her make-up kit, she was not in the habit of using it or beautifying herself in front of others, lest the women misunderstand her. *There must be a mirror somewhere, and definitely so in the drawing room.* She went into the drawing room and saw her reflection in the life-size mirror there. There was no one in the room at that time. The men were out in the courtyard, and the women were busy singing. She minutely scrutinized each part of her body. She could not spot a single blemish either on her face or in her entire form. But the former freshness, the seductive attraction and the loveliness was missing. Surely, it was absent. She could not delude herself. But what was the reason for this unfortunate lack? Perhaps Ramdulari's youth had just blossomed whereas her own had withered a long time ago. But this thought could not pacify the conflict in her mind. She could not live eclipsed thus by Ramdulari. Men are such blockheads! None among them has the ability to assess true beauty. They are just after youthful flatteries and overexcitement. They fail to see, despite having eyes. What have these to do with real beauty? Beauty is nine days' wonder. True beauty transcends time.

If Ramdulari were to dress up in Rupkumari's clothes, all the magic of her beauty would disappear. She would look like a hideous witch. Who could make these foolish men understand all this? But the family that Ramdulari had married into was not very well off. Indeed, the clothes and jewellery that had come from her in-laws at the time of the wedding was very disappointing. Besides, there was nothing that could have indicated or assured her future happiness. Her father-in-law was a public attorney of a state, while the groom was merely studying in a college. So from where could she have found such a windfall during these last two years that could explain her prosperity? Who knows—maybe she had borrowed the jewellery from someone? And she might have borrowed her clothes as well. Some women have the habit of pretending to be richer and better off than they really are. *Let such pretensions remain with Ramdulari. I am better off the way I am.*

The fever of fashion is increasing every day. There may not be sufficient food to eat at home, with the husband earning no more than twenty-five to thirty rupees from quill driving, but the wife comes out of her home, all dressed up, as if she were some princess. She would bear the complaints of tailors and cloth dealers, the frowns and volleys of angry words hurled by her husband, she would weep or become annoyed—but nothing would dissuade her from continuing to make a fashion statement. Even family members might be laughing at her pretentious ways, but she was clearly too unashamed and stood unmoved by any such criticism. No matter how much one laughed at her, she was far too shameless to give any heed to it. She just aimed at attracting men whenever she appeared in the public. Ramdulari must have borrowed her jewels and dress from someone, the shameless woman that she is!

Now Rupkumari's sense of self-respect brightened her face. So what if she had no jewels and good clothes; she need not hang her head in shame in front of anyone. She need not hide her face from anyone. Her real treasures were her two sons. May God bless them with long lives! Her happiness lay in their welfare. Merely having good food and good clothes for oneself is not the main source of fulfilment in one's life. No doubt she came from a poor family, but they were well respected; they were not unjust to anyone, nor did anybody curse them.

She went out again into the veranda after cheering herself up in this manner. Once she was there, she noticed Ramdulari looking at her with pity.

Ramdulari asked, 'Has your husband been promoted, sister, or is he still rotting on seventy-five rupees?'

Rupkumari's heart was on fire. 'Such pride!' she whispered to herself, as if Ramdulari's own husband was a lord. She retorted arrogantly, 'Of course he got a promotion! He is now in the hundred-rupee grade. One should be thankful for this. These days, even people who have qualified MAs can hardly get a job. Your husband must be pursuing his BA, is he not?

Ramdulari snorted and said, 'He left his studies, sister! Further education would've only marred his prospects. He works as an agent in a company and earns two hundred and fifty rupees per month, along with some commission. He also gets five rupees per day as travelling expenditure. In a way, his income is roughly five hundred rupees every month. He spends almost a hundred and fifty rupees on his own self, sister. A person in such a high position has to maintain a suitable standard of life. Out of the remaining amount of three hundred and fifty rupees, I get a hundred for my personal expenditures, and the household is managed smoothly from the remaining two hundred and fifty rupees. What would have he done by passing his MA examination?'

For a moment, Rupkumari suspected that Ramdulari was telling her tall tales, but Ramdulari's expression exuded confidence and a sense of failure was clearly apparent on Rupkumari's face. But Rupkumari knew that if she did not want to lose her sanity completely, she would have to first extinguish the fire of jealousy in her heart. Hence, as a way of reassuring herself, she decided to concede that only one-fourth of whatever Ramdulari had said was true; anything more than that would have been too unbearable for Rupkumari to accept. However, at the same time, her heartbeat raced at the nagging fear that what Ramdulari had said might be the actual truth. She was afraid she might burst into tears at any moment. What a great difference there was between the seventy-five rupees that her husband earned and the income of five hundred rupees of Ramdulari's husband! She could not reconcile herself to the huge figure even if it were possible to earn that much as a result of self-abasement. At most, one's self can be valued at a hundred, but not five-hundred at any rate!

Mockingly, Rupkumari asked, 'Well, now that agents are earning so much money and other allowances, why don't all the colleges shut down? Why are thousands of boys wasting their lives in higher studies?'

Ramdulari, who was inwardly drawing pleasure from her sister's discomfiture, responded, 'Sister, now you are making a mistake. Anyone can get through the MA examination, but only a few can work as agents. It's God's gift. One may study for a lifetime, but it's not necessary that he can work effectively as an agent. To be a scholar is one thing, but moneymaking is a different thing altogether. It is not easy to win the customer's confidence about the quality of your products and to convince them that you're selling the cheap and best wares! As an agent, he has to deal with all sorts of customers. One has to perform convincingly before rich men—only then do goods get traded. These rich men and nobles are inaccessible to an ordinary person; and if by some stroke of luck, such a person happens to gain access to their presence, he is unable to speak, almost boggled. In the beginning, my husband also used to hesitate, but now he is as clever as a crocodile in his trade. Next year, he is going to get a promotion.'

It was as though the blood in Rupkumari's veins had ceased to flow. Why doesn't the cruel sky fall down and the stone-hearted earth explode at such brutal injustice? What kind of justice was it that, Rupkumari—who was so beautiful, well mannered, hard-working, so devoted to her husband and affectionate to her children that she valued them more than her life, so economical that she managed the household within the meagre earnings—should be in such a pitiable condition, whereas Ramdulari—who was proud, arrogant, impolite, a pleasure seeker and an impulsive girl who used to roam around with untidy hair—was now living like a queen? Yet, there was a faint trace of hope left in her. Perhaps she would find a way to regain her peace of mind in the future.

Then Rupkumari replied mockingly, 'So, perhaps your husband will start getting a thousand rupees?'

'Not a thousand rupees, but undoubtedly six hundred.'

'Some befuddled employer must have been caught in this trap!'

'Businessmen are no fools, sister! They are far wiser than you and me. If you give them a benefit of six thousand rupees, only then are you likely to get six hundred. Who can fool the likes of those who are experts in fooling the whole world?'

Seeing that mere sarcasm was not working, Rupkumari deployed the weapon of insult, and argued, 'I don't consider it a very good profession. For the whole day, one primarily lies and cheats. It is nothing but trickery.'

Ramdulari laughed loudly. She realized that she had completely overwhelmed her sister.

'In that way, all lawyers and barristers too are cheats. What do they not do for their clients? They even have to create false evidence. But we make the same lawyers and barristers our leaders, elect them as presidents of our national conferences, pull their vehicles, shower flowers and gold coins on them, name roads, institutions and build statues after them. Today, the world reveres money. It has always been like that. No one bothers to think about the means by which the money is earned. Whoever has money is worshipped, whereas people who are unfortunate, incapable and incompetent, console themselves with the idea of spirituality and righteousness. But who really cares about such virtues?'

At this, Rupkumari fell silent. Now she had to admit to the truth, with all its pain and agony, that Ramdulari was more fortunate than her. Now there was no escape. To continue criticizing and insulting Ramdulari would yield no fruit; rather, it would only exhibit her own narrowness of mind. Now she had to visit Ramdulari's house on some pretext to find out the reality. If Lakshmi, the Goddess of wealth, had blessed Ramdulari, then Rupkumari had no option but to grieve over her own misfortune. She would understand that justice did not exist in this world and that honesty had no value.

But would this explanation satisfy her? And in any case, who was honest in this world? Only the person who could not grab an opportunity to act dishonestly or the one who was not intelligent enough to create such an opportunity. Her husband, who earned seventy-five rupees only, wouldn't he feel happy to get ten or twenty rupees more? He would remain honest and truthful only until the moment he found an opportunity to become corrupt. His whole truthfulness would evaporate at the first temptation which might come along his way. Moreover, was Rupkumari morally strong enough to prevent her husband from using the ill-gotten gains? Far from stopping him, she would be pleased instead. Perhaps she may even pat her husband's back in encouragement. Presently, she sits without any enthusiastic anticipation of her husband returning home from the office. Then, closer to his return, she keeps a vigil at the door, awaiting his arrival, and the moment he reached, she would start searching his pockets.

There was singing in the courtyard. Ramdulari was singing joyously. Rupkumari was sitting disconsolate on the veranda. Who knows why her head had started aching? Whether someone was singing or dancing, Rupkumari was indifferent to the cheerful environment. She was unfortunate, born only to weep.

The guests started leaving at nine. Rupkumari also got up. She was going to order a horse cart when Ramdulari said, 'Sister, why send for a horse cart? My car must be coming here to take me home. Spend four or five days at my home before returning to your own. I shall send a message to your husband not to wait for you.'

And so Rupkumari's last weapon also failed. She now lost all desire to find out the reality of Ramdulari's household situation. Now she would go to her own home and cover her face, and lie down, brooding. And, how could she visit her sister's house in such shabby clothes?

Rupkumari said, 'No, I am not free right now. The children must be worried. I shall come some other day.'

'Won't you stay even for a single night?'

'No.'

'Okay, please tell me when you can come. I shall send you the car.'

'I will let you know.'

'You will forget. A year passed and you did not care enough to remember me, even by mistake, and I was waiting to receive an invitation from you. Even though we live in the same city, we don't see each other for months.'

Rupkumari had no other option but to say that her home kept her very busy and that she had thought of inviting Ramdulari quite a few times, but failed to find an opportunity to do so.

Just then Ramdulari's husband, Gurusevak, arrived and greeted his sister-in-law. Dressed exactly like an Englishman, a cigar in his mouth, a gold watch on his wrist and gold-framed spectacles shielding his eyes, as if he was a civilian. His face exhibited gentlemanliness and worldly wisdom. Rupkumari had never imagined he would be so handsome. His clothes fitted him very well indeed.

Blessing him, Rupkumari said, 'How could I have met you had I not come here today!'

Gurusevak said laughingly, 'You are wrongly blaming me. Did you ever invite me home and I did not come?'

'I never thought you would consider yourself a guest in my house, for it is as much yours.'

Ramdulari was watching how, despite being jealous in her heart, Rupkumari was speaking in such a sweet, affectionate and courteous tone.

Gurusevak replied in a generous tone, 'Now I agree, *bhabhi sahib*. It is certainly my fault. I never thought that way. But you have to stay at my home today.'

'No, today I have no time. I'll come some other day. The boys must be getting anxious.'

Ramdulari said, 'I too requested her a lot, but she just doesn't agree.'

Eventually, both the sisters seated themselves in the rear seat of the car, while Gurusevak drove. In a few minutes, they reached the house. Ramdulari again requested her sister to stay the night, but her efforts were in vain. After all, the children would be anxious. At last, Ramdulari hugged her and took leave. Gurusevak carried on driving. Rupkumari cast a fleeting glance on Ramdulari's house and the true fact of prosperity cut her to the quick.

After covering a little distance, Gurusevak said, 'Bhabhi, I have chosen a good career for myself. If the work continues to progress like this for three or four years, I will become a prosperous man.'

Rupkumari said sympathetically, 'Ramdulari told me. May God keep you happy wherever you are. But you should move ahead cautiously.'

'Bhabhi, I consider it a sin to take even a single rupee without the knowledge of my employer. One can enjoy wealth only when it is honestly earned. To earn money at the cost of one's respect is of no value. I consider such wealth unworthy. Further, who do I have to fear? I'm in charge of the whole operation. My employer is no more, only his widow lives and she has entrusted the charge of everything to me. Had I not managed the affairs of her business, she would have lost it. It was my third month in the business when my employer passed away. But he knew how to assess a person. I was hired at a hundred rupees, but the very next month, my salary was hiked to two hundred. With all your blessings, I amplified the business to the tune of twelve thousand in the very first month.'

Without any motive, Rupkumari asked, 'What is the nature of your work?'

'I work as an agent where different types of machines are imported and later sold,' he replied calmly.

They reached Rupkumari's dingy house. A lantern was dimly lit outside the door. Her husband, Umanath, was strolling at the door. But Rupkumari did not insist Gurusevak to come out of the car—she only invited him in once, merely as a formality. And as for Umanath, he did not even bother to greet Gurusevak.

Rupkumari's house felt a graveyard to her now, a symbol of misfortune. There was no flooring, nor any furniture or flower pots. All it had were a few broken stools, a broken table and some old cots. Till that morning, Rupkumari had been happy in that house. But now, it was grating on her nerves. The boys yelled out in excitement, 'Mother, Mother!' and ran towards her but she indifferently scolded them. Her head was aching. She wouldn't talk to anyone nor would she entertain any kind of disturbance. Dinner was still uncooked.

Who else would have cooked it? The children had had milk, but Umanath hadn't taken anything yet. He was waiting for Rupkumari to return and cook. But Rupkumari's head was aching. So the only option left was to get puris from the market.

Rupkumari asked angrily, 'Why were you waiting for me till now? I wasn't brought here as your cook! And what if I had stayed there at night? Why don't you keep a cook? Or would you keep grinding me all my life?'

Startled and hurt, Umanath looked at his wife, unable to decipher the reason for her unusual behaviour. He had always received wholehearted cooperation from her. Not only cooperation, but also unstinting support. In fact, he had himself proposed many times that they engage a cook, but she would constantly refuse by saying, 'What will I do sitting idle? Why should we add an unnecessary expense of four or five rupees? That much money could be spent in getting butter for the children.'

And today, she was spitefully taunting him, as if filled with resentment.

Defending himself, he said, 'I've suggested to you several times that we should keep a cook.'

'Then why didn't you engage one? If I had turned her out once she was appointed, then you could complain!'

'Well, then I'm at fault.'

'You never proposed this wholeheartedly,' Rupkumari retorted more angrily. 'You only said this to please me. I am not such a simpleton that I don't understand your inner motives. You never thought of my comfort. You were happy to have a servant at your disposal, one who was satisfied with little food and a few clothes, and that too, when there was some money left over after all the household expenses. You place the petty amount of seventy-five rupees in my hand, out of which I am supposed to manage all sorts of expenses. Only I know how I make both ends meet. I am troubled with the thought of what I should wear! You have ruined my life! There are men in this world who pluck stars from the sky for the sake of their wives' happiness. Why go far, look at Gurusevak! He is less educated than you are and even younger than you, but still earns five hundred rupees a month and Ramdulari lives like a queen. But you are satisfied with the petty amount of seventy-five rupees, and busy in your own world. What kind of a man are you, you should've been born a woman. A woman's heart is filled with countless desires and wishes. But you are not bothered about me. You have no problems. You want to have good food to eat and good clothes to wear just because you are a man, the sole earner, but you don't give a damn about how I exist.'

This verbal volley of abuses continued for a few minutes while Umanath remained silent. In his whole life, he had never given Rupkumari a chance to complain. It was undeniable that he got only a small amount as salary, but he was helpless in this matter. He did his work faithfully and tried his best to stay in the good books of his officers. This year, he had taught the head officer's younger son for six months without a break only to please him. What else could he do? He understood the reason behind Rupkumari's rage. If Gurusevak was indeed drawing five hundred rupees as salary, then he was definitely a fortunate man. But one does not break one's head at other's good fortune! Gurusevak might have been fortunate enough to get this opportunity, but not everyone was so lucky. He would investigate whether Gurusevak was actually getting five hundred rupees or was it just a hoax. But even if he was getting that much money, how did it give Rupkumari the right to insult and abuse Umanath? What if he too started abusing and taunting his wife the same way, finding a more beautiful and generous woman? Of course, Rupkumari was beautiful, soft-spoken and self-sacrificing, but surely there are other women in the whole world who surpass her in all these qualities? So should he start disrespecting her for this reason?

There was a time when no other woman was as beautiful as Rupkumari in his eyes in the whole world. But that feeling no longer existed. A long time had passed since he had emerged from that romantic world into a more practical one. Now, he had gained experience of married life. They were now familiar with each other's virtues and flaws. Contentment was the only way for them to stay happy. But Rupkumari, despite being wise, had failed to understand such a simple truth.

Still, he sympathized with Rupkumari. He was good-hearted and an imaginative person. So, he remained silent at Rupkumari's angry outburst and swallowed it without complaint. It was natural for Rupkumari to get disturbed for a moment seeing the lavishness of her sister's life. Rupkumari was no ascetic or self-denying person to stay happy under every condition.

Convincing himself thus, Umanath resolved to investigate the matters of Gurusevak.

2

For about a week, Rupkumari remained distraught.

She would get irritated at every trifle, scold the boys, curse her husband and bemoan her fate. She did the household chores as usual, but not wholeheartedly; now they seemed a burden to her. She was no longer preoccupied with the cleaning and maintenance of those things that she had once developed an emotional attachment with and upon which she used to lavish so much attention. There was only one servant in the house. When he saw that Rupkumari hardly cared about managing the household, why should he bother to clean it? Chaos and disorder ruled the house—who would care to bring order? The children were afraid of talking to their mother, whereas Umanath would evade her very shadow. Whatever was served, Umanath would silently gulp it down and leave for his office. After returning from the office, he would take both his children for a walk. Speaking to Rupkumari was like wilfully setting a spark to an explosive. But his investigation of Gurusevak continued.

One day, when Umanath returned from his office, Gurusevak was accompanying him. That day, after many days, Rupkumari had finally reconciled with the situation and was dusting chairs and tables, when Gurusevak entered and greeted her. She burnt with anger upon seeing him with Umanath and bit back the urge to scratch her husband's face. Why had he brought Gurusevak home with no prior notice? What would Gurusevak be thinking after seeing her in this condition? But Umanath had always lacked brains. Despite all her efforts to conceal her sad plight, Umanath was himself exposing the reality of their circumstances. He was shameless. Who knows what she had done to Umanath for him to keep on insulting her?

After giving him her blessings, she asked Gurusevak after the well-being of his family and offered him a chair to sit. Sitting down, he said, 'Today *bhai sahib* has invited me home. I would not have come on his invitation but when he said that you were insisting, I spared some time to come here.'

Rupkumari diverted him by saying, 'That day I couldn't talk to you as I was preoccupied.'

Gurusevak, glancing around the room, remarked, 'You must be facing great difficulty living in this cage.'

Rupkumari realized that he was very inconsiderate and insensitive, with no regard for others' feelings. She thought, *He doesn't even understand that not all people are fortunate enough in this world. Only one among lakhs is lucky, and if it were not so, how else would he stand out as an exception, as the fortunate one? Where most people don't even have enough to eat, what greatness could there be in the pleasure and prosperity of the few? In contrast, their extravagance is a sign of their impudence and insolence rather than of their fortune.'*

Irritated, she said, 'It is better to live in a cage rather than in a big house, for in the cage, the birds live in harmony, while a spacious place befits the dwelling of fierce animals.'

Perhaps Gurusevak could not catch the drift; he said, 'I'd feel suffocated in this house. I'll arrange a spacious house for you in my neighbourhood. You'll not have to pay any rent, for it belongs to the widow of my employer. I also live in one of her houses. She has hundreds of such houses. All of them are under my charge. It is entirely my discretion to give any of them on rent or for free. I'll get the best one repaired for you because of my love and respect for you.'

Rupkumari understood that he was inebriated; that was why he was talking nonsense. On closer inspection, she found his cheeks swollen and his eyes getting smaller. He was stammering as well. She began to loathe his handsome, smart and innocent face which had turned shameless and brazen because of his bragging.

After a moment, he started babbling again. 'I respect you a lot, for you are my *Badi Bhabhi*. I am always at your service. Not only one, but a hundred houses could be at your disposal. I am Mrs Lohia's attorney. Everything is in my hands—everything! Whatever I say she accepts blindly. She considers me her son. I am the owner of all her property. Mr Lohia employed me for just twenty rupees, just twenty rupees! He was very rich. But no one knew the secret of his wealth except me.

'He was a smuggler. Don't tell anyone! He sold cocaine secretly and earned lakhs of rupees. I'm doing the same business now. We have our secret agents in every city. Working under Mr Lohia has made me an expert in this business. No one dares arrest me, for I am securely in the good books of all the higher officials. I silence them with bundles of money. No one can utter a word. I sell drugs openly. I write in the accounts that I paid a thousand rupees as a bribe, whereas I had actually paid five hundred only—the rest is for me and my friends. Money is limitless and I spend extravagantly. I am not accountable to anyone. The old woman is engrossed in prayers all the time. After devouring so many mice, the cat is now seeking salvation!'

Taking a bundle of notes from his pocket, he continued, 'Take this as my token of love to you and bless me that I should live my whole life in the same luxurious manner. Whoever thinks of the soul and righteousness is eventually abandoned by Kuber, the Lord of wealth. And Lakshmi, the

Goddess of wealth, showers her blessings only upon those who renounce their religion and honesty for her sake. Don't get me wrong. I am not that rich. All the wealthy men are robbers and dacoits. If tomorrow, I get fortunate enough and build a dharmashala, I will be praised and admired by all. Who cares how I earn the money? I can hire any priest to sing my praises. Mr Lohia, who was an unsurpassed sinner, was given the title of *Dharmabhushan*, the ornament of religion, by priests—those selfish, material worshippers. This hypocrisy rules the day. A lawyer earns five hundred rupees in a half-hour argument, a doctor pockets a thousand rupees by giving a simple injection, and a gambler exacts lakhs in a day. If their income is legal, then mine is too.'

'In my eyes, there is no respect for even the wealthiest of them. I know their tricks. The one who is a master swindler is successful. Becoming rich by robbing poor people is the oldest tradition of our society. I am also doing the same and this is my life's sole aim. I will rob as much as possible and enjoy limitless wealth and will give large sums of money in charity in my old age, and one day I will become a leader. Should I count how many people have become rich through gambling and trafficking women?'

Suddenly, Umanath came in and said, 'Mr Gurusevak, what are you doing? Come and have your tea. It is getting cold.'

Gurusevak was startled and tried to stabilize himself in order to act normal. But his legs faltered and he fell down. Then he collected himself to stand up, and staggering and stumbling all the while, went out of the room.

Rupkumari heaved a sigh of relief. She felt suffocated, as if the air in the room was nauseating. The ugliness of the things that had attracted and fascinated her a few days ago were now revealed in their stark reality. The entry of such ideas like selfishness, dishonesty and trickery in her life—till now lived with simplicity, sacrifice and devotion—was akin to the invasion of a herd of bulls into a garden. She did not want worldly pleasures and riches at such a heavy cost. No, not at all. Now she would never compare her fate with that of Ramdulari's. She was happy with her lot. She pitied Ramdulari as she was selling her soul for material pleasures. But her sister was also helpless and Gurusevak could not be blamed either. Apparently, the fault rested not with them, but rather with society where wealth was worshipped so outrageously, where a person's worth was assessed by his bank accounts and lavish lifestyle; where temptation ruled at every step, and where base thoughts of jealousy, hate and exploitation were flagrantly encouraged. And it should not surprise one if Ramdulari and Gurusevak too were driven by the same pressures.

Just then Umanath asked his wife, 'What was Gurusevak blabbering about? I bade him farewell lest the police may be after him. Otherwise, I too would have been in trouble.'

Rupkumari replied in an ashamed tone, 'He was bragging about his smuggling business.'

'He even asked me to meet Mrs Lohia.'

'No, you better stick to your clerkship. We are better off as we are.'

'But a clerkship does not offer such luxuries. Why not take leave for one year and experience the pleasures of Gurusevak's world?'

'All such luxuries don't attract me any more.'

'Are you serious?'

'Yes, wholeheartedly.'

After a minute's silence, Umanath spoke again, 'Had I told you the same story, would you have believed me or not? Tell me honestly.'

'No, never. I could've never imagined that anyone can dispense poison to others in order to benefit himself.'

'I found out the whole story from the sub-inspector. I made Gurusevak drink heavily so that he would vomit the truth himself in his inebriated state.'

'Perhaps you too were tempted.'

'Yes, I was tempted. I still am. But where would I learn the shrewdness required to earn in this business?'

'God forbid you should never learn such skills. I pity that poor man. I don't know whether he reached home safely.'

'Don't worry. He left in his own car.'

Rupkumari stared at the ground for a moment and said, 'Take me to Ramdulari's home. I might be of some help to her. The garden of pleasure in which she is strolling in right now is surrounded by demons on all sides. Maybe I can save her.'

Umanath saw that Rupkumari's visage was brimming with pity and concern for her sister.

Translated from the Hindi by
Shaifta Ayoub and Kalyanee Rajan

A Positive Change

1

There was a village by the name of Beera in the Patna region. An old, helpless Gond woman known as Bhungi lived there. She didn't have an inch of land or a home to live in. She only had a parching oven. The villagers were accustomed to having just one meal a day of parched grains or gram flour. That's why there was always a crowd around Bhungi's oven. She ate whatever grains she earned from parching the grains of others. Sometimes she ground them and ate the powder. She slept in a corner of the shack beside the oven. She woke up early in the morning to gather dry leaves from all around to light the oven. One always saw a mound of leaves close to the oven. She lit the oven in the afternoon. But on Ekadashi and Poornmasi, the oven was not lit, and on the days when Thakur Veer Singh, the zamindar of the village, ordered her to parch his grains, she had to go to bed hungry. Not only did she have to parch Thakur's grains free of cost, she also had to fetch water for his household. She lived in his village and, hence, he had the right to extract work from her without payment. This could not be considered injustice. The only injustice was that he never gave her a tip. He felt that if he had to pay her something, then what was the point of unpaid labour? After all, the farmer had the right to make his oxen work the field the entire day and then tether them to the pole without giving them fodder. And if he did not do that, it was not because of his kindness but because of sheer necessity. Thakur, in principle, was averse to paying wages. He had no concern for Bhungi because she wouldn't die even if she went hungry for an entire day. Old people did not die so easily; they were adept at giving the slip to the Angel of Death. And, God forbid, even if she chose to kick the bucket then, in her place, another Gond woman could easily be installed at the parching oven.

2

It was the month of Chait and was one day before the festival of Sankranti. That day, in Bihar and other districts, people partook of gram flour from newly harvested grains and also gave it away as alms. People had not lit the stoves in their homes. Bhungi's oven was teeming with people. She didn't have a moment to spare. She was getting annoyed with customers for showing undue haste and said, 'I've just one pair of hands, not two. And if I don't parch the grains well, you'll call me names!' In the meantime, two big baskets of grains arrived from the thakur's house with the order to parch them immediately. Bhungi was alarmed. It was already afternoon, and it was difficult to parch all the grains before sunset. If she had had one or two more hours of work, she could have earned enough grains to last the following eight days. But

God didn't show her this much pity. Instead, He sent her
these angels of death! Now she had to burn herself at the
oven through the night. On top of it, they'd find fault with
her for no reason—'the grains have decreased in amount',
'you haven't parched them enough', 'you've parched them
too hard', 'you've taken too much time'. She put aside both
baskets despairingly.

The servant warned her, 'Don't be late, you'll regret it.'

Bhungi replied, 'You can sit here and wait. When I finish
parching, take them along. Chop off my hands if I touch
anybody else's grain before finishing yours.'

'We don't have permission to sit here, but see to it that
they're roasted by evening.' Warning her, the servant went
away and Bhungi started parching the grains. The other
customers raised a clamour: 'We've been waiting for two
hours and you haven't parched our grains. How will we have
flour tomorrow?'

Bhungi said peevishly, 'What can I do? It's Thakur's job.
If I don't do it where will I live? Didn't you have a tongue
in your head? Why didn't you ask his servants that if they
dumped such a huge quantity of grain on me, how could I
parch yours?'

Helpless, people picked up their baskets and walked
away. Bhungi became busy in her work with frantic energy.
But it was no joke to parch grains weighing about a maund,
especially when during the course of the work one had to
leave the roasting and rake the embers to keep the oven
warm. By late evening she hadn't finished even half the work.
She feared that the zamindar's servants would be on their
way. And as soon as they arrived they'd start abusing her. She
became even more frantic. Her gaze was fixed on the doorway

while she kept working the oven. The sand cooled down and the grains came up half-parched. Her hands were frozen from working the heavy iron ladle continuously. She didn't know what to do and began to weep. 'I don't know why God has forsaken me! So many people die every day, even death has forgotten me. Those who suffer in this world aren't shown any mercy in the other world too. Who cares for me? I shed my blood to earn some grains. But Thakur is always after my life, simply because I live in his village. Is this small patch of land worth so much? There are so many plots that lie fallow in the village, so many households that lie deserted. Those lands do not produce *kesar*, then why should I live under threat all the time? And at the slightest excuse they threaten to dig up my oven and throw me away. If I had somebody to protect me then I wouldn't have to put up with their threats.'

She was engrossed in such thoughts when the two servants arrived and asked, 'Have you roasted the grains?'

Bhungi said fearlessly, 'I'm doing it. Can't you see?'

'The whole day is over and you haven't yet finished parching the grains? And are you parching the grains or just wasting them! These are just half-parched, how will anyone make flour out of them? Just wait and watch how the thakur deals with you today.'

The consequence was that the same night the oven was pulled out and the hapless widow was left without shelter.

3

Bhungi had no means of livelihood now. With the destruction of the oven the villagers also were much inconvenienced.

Many families had to go without food during lunch. The people went to Thakur and pleaded with him to allow Bhungi to run the oven, but he couldn't care less. 'She's a devil and a pig-headed crone. She'll come to her senses if she has to starve for a couple of days. She has spoilt a sackful of my grains. Must be thinking what harm can I do her! She doesn't know that it is because of me that she has been living here peacefully.' Hearing these harsh words from Thakur the people went back to their homes.

One of them said, 'Why show his authority to a woman who's almost dead? He should show it to someone who is his equal.'

A second one said, 'All his authority consists of exploiting the poor. He trembles at the sight of the government emissaries; what to speak of his peers. Well, we live in his village. He can treat us the way he likes.'

Bhungi somehow managed to pass some days. She had earned more grains on the day of Sankranti. When they finished she began to starve. Several people advised her to go to another village and settle down. 'We'll go there to build a shack where you can run your oven. You can stay in peace. All zamindars aren't alike.' But Bhungi didn't agree. She had spent fifty years of her difficult life in that village. She had fallen in love with each tree and plant of the village. She knew all the children of the village and they also knew her. The entire village seemed like her house. She had seen many ups and downs in her life in that village. Now, at the very end of her life, she couldn't sever her connection with it! The mere thought of it seemed to give her pain. She would rather stay and suffer in that village than leave it for the comforts of another.

An entire month passed in this way. It was early in the morning. Thakur Veer Singh, along with two or three of his servants, was going around collecting taxes. He didn't trust his agents, and didn't want to share the customary gifts of money given by tenants to a landlord. Sometimes he'd say, 'What's left in being a landlord? After paying off the government and the expenses of the court, one is left with less than ten rupees out of a hundred. We can't but depend on extra income for all the pomp and show.' He looked around himself arrogantly, smiled at the greetings of his subjects and walked away. He had great authority and was held in awe by his subjects. Women used to draw their veils and turn away their faces at the sight of him. People sitting on doorsteps stood up in his honour, adjusting their turbans. Some concealed their coconuts from his sight. Wandering around the village with such swagger he walked past Bhungi's oven. As his gaze fell on the oven he was filled with rage. The oven was being made anew. The old woman was placing heaps of clay on it swiftly. She had probably started working in the dead of the night and wanted to finish it off before sunrise. It was the day of the deity's worship. As per custom, Bhungi wanted to feed *sattu* to all the unmarried girls of the village on her *chabutara*. She always parched grains in her oven on this occasion. She didn't charge anything for her labour. If the oven was not ready that day how would she parch the grains? If the grains are parched in some other village the deity might get angry and the village might be visited by some calamity. If the thakur got angry, it didn't matter. The deity must be pleased. If the thakur was displeased the worst he could do was dig up the oven. However, if the deity was displeased, the entire village would suffer. The thakur himself was a devotee of the Goddess; he wouldn't dare act against her wishes. Even the king is scared of the Goddess, what to speak of Thakur? These thoughts led her to repair the oven. She was so lost in her work that she didn't realize the presence of the thakur. Suddenly, she heard a voice say, 'Who gave you permission?'

Startled, Bhungi looked up to see Thakur standing in front of her. She couldn't reply.

Thakur repeated his question, 'Who gave you permission?'

Bhungi answered fearlessly, 'The deity.'

'I'm the owner of this village, not the deity,' Thakur thundered.

Bhungi touched her heart with her hands and said, 'Thakur, don't utter such words. The deity is the owner of the whole world, what to speak of you and me.'

Thakur said to his servants, 'What a cantankerous old woman! She wants to scare me in the name of the deity and lower my status in the eyes of others. Smash her oven.'

His servants didn't dare do this. Thakur was now furious. He called his servants all kinds of names, got down from the horse and gave a mighty kick to the oven. The clay was still wet, it flattened out. As he aimed a second kick, the old woman stood right in front of him and it fell on her back. She stumbled to the ground with her face down. Now, she was also angry. She stroked her back with one hand and said, 'Thakur, if you don't fear humans at least fear the gods and deities. What will you gain by destroying me thus? Will you dig up gold from this palm-sized land? I'm saying this for your own good. The curse of the poor will harm you. Don't hurt me so much.'

Thakur asked, 'I hope you won't want to build an oven here again.'

'What will I eat if I don't build an oven?'

'It is not my responsibility to provide for you. Get out of the village.'

'Why should I go? If a subject ploughs a piece of land for twelve years he becomes a shareholder. I have turned old living in this hut. My father and mother-in-law and their fathers and forefathers all have lived in this very hut. Now only Yamdoot[1] can take me away from here.'

'So now you are displaying your knowledge of the law. If you had begged and pleaded I might have allowed you to stay, but now I shan't have a moment's peace until I've turned you out.' (To the servants.) 'Go now and set fire to the heap of leaves. Let's see how she ignites the oven.'

'Today we're offering puja to the deity. Let me light the oven. Do whatever you want tomorrow.'

'You think there's only your oven in the world? Other villages too have ovens.'

4

In an instant sparks began to fly and the flames rose up to touch the sky. They also began to spread on all sides. The villagers gathered and stood around that mountain of fire. Bhungi was sitting dejectedly near the oven and watching the heart-rending scene. No one knew what thoughts ran through her mind. *Such anger against me! All because of this hapless belly. A curse on such a life! Who's there to call my own that I should bear with all this just to remain alive? What support do I have now? The oven lies smashed. The leaves have turned to ash. Shall*

---

[1] Angel of Death.

I now resort to begging to fill my belly? I have lived most of my life without stretching my hand before anyone. Shall I now live to be pushed around as today? These thoughts brought tears to her eyes. She was overcome by her helplessness and longing. She felt dizzy. Suddenly she ran and jumped into the fire. People came running from all directions but nobody showed the courage to go into the mouth of fire. Thakur was sitting on his horse and watching the scene. The moment Bhungi entered the fire he jumped like lightning from his horse and in an instant entered the flames. The crowd was stunned and stood there with bated breath. In no time Thakur came out holding Bhungi in his lap. His clothes had caught fire. Bhungi's clothes, too, were in flames. She was unconscious. People took off the blankets they were wearing and put them around Thakur. Nobody bothered about Bhungi. They were all busy looking after Thakur. Luckily, the fire didn't cause any harm to his body, only his skin was scorched in places. But Bhungi's body was badly burnt.

Half an hour passed. The flames were still burning. Thakur still held Bhungi in his lap as tears trickled down his face. The women of his house had also arrived there. Someone was fanning Bhungi while someone else was applying balm on her injuries. Others were suggesting home remedies.

Suddenly, Thakur said, 'Send someone to the city to bring a doctor immediately.'

His wife said, 'She'll be all right with the help of home remedies. Why should you call in a doctor?'

'If she dies I'll drink poison.'

'She won't die now.'

Thakur said eagerly, 'Yes, if I have my way, she won't die of shock. She'll die a natural death.'

5

Thakur Veer Singh was not known to be a nice person in his area. This event made him popular with the high and the low. All his subjects praised him for his valour. But his fellow zamindars termed it as a temporary loss of judgement. To them, it was pointless to jump into fire for such an old woman. Her death wouldn't have made the world bereft. She had no one in the world to cry over her. But if the zamindar had died, he would have left his family without an heir.

A month had passed. Bhungi was lying down in Thakur's house and Thakur was sitting beside her bed. Bhungi said, 'Brother, I've recovered now. Why don't you allow me to run my oven? How long will I stay here? It's been a long time.'

Thakur said, 'Sister, are you bored? Do you have any discomfort here?'

Bhungi replied, 'Yes, brother. I'm bored. Won't one get bored eating goodies and staying idle all day long? What discomfort can be greater than this? Brother, didn't you feel any fear when you jumped into the fire after me? Why should you have risked your life for an old woman? I always wonder what thoughts ran through your mind at that moment.'

Thakur said, 'I had no time to think. It was as though I was in a trance. I was not myself. My steps advanced towards the fire automatically. I didn't care what I was doing and why. It was as though I had lost my senses. Everything happened on its own. God wanted to save me from disgrace. What else?'

Translated from the Urdu by M. Asaduddin

The Condemned

1

Orphaned early and a widow now, Maani had nothing to fall back on except her tears. She was only five when her father died. At sixteen, her mother, who had somehow raised her, managed to get her married off with the help of the neighbours. But within a year, Maani lost both her mother and her husband. In this crisis, she could think of no one who could give her shelter except her uncle Vanshidhar. So far, Vanshidhar had behaved in a manner that left little hope for a peaceful existence with him. But she was ready to endure anything. She would tolerate all his abuses, scolding and beatings. At least no one would suspect or accuse her falsely of any wrongdoing. She would be protected from scoundrels and ruffians. Vanshidhar, somewhat concerned about his family honour, was unable to turn down Maani's request.

But within a month or two Maani realized she would not be able to survive in this place for long. She did all the housework, danced to everyone's tune and tried to keep everyone happy, but for some unknown reason, her uncle and aunt remained bitter. They got rid of the maidservant the moment Maani arrived. Even the boy who used to wash and clean was dismissed. But in spite of all this relief, her uncle and aunt didn't treat her with kindness. Chacha directed threats at her, chachi called her names and her cousin Lalita cursed her at any given opportunity. In the entire household, only her cousin Gokul was sympathetic towards her. Only his words conveyed to her a sense of closeness and affection. Gokul knew his mother's nature. If he tried to make her understand the situation or supported Maani openly, she would have found it impossible to continue living in the house. That is why his sympathy remained limited to just comforting Maani. He would say, 'Sister, let me get a job and that will be the end of your troubles. Then I will see who looks at you with scorn. Your bad times will last only as long I am a student.' Maani would be thrilled at these words of affection, and she would bless Gokul from every pore of her being.

2

It was the day of Lalita's wedding. Guests had been pouring in since morning. The house resounded with the jingle of ornaments. Seeing the guests Maani too felt elated. She had no ornaments on her body, she had not received any pretty dresses, yet her face was brimming with joy.

It was the middle of the night; the auspicious hour for the nuptials had arrived. Gifts for the bride had come from the groom's quarters. Women were restless with curiosity to catch a glimpse of the gifts. Lalita was being adorned with ornaments. Maani had an intense desire to go and see the bride.

She could not resist the craving to see yesterday's little girl transformed into a bride. Smilingly, she entered the room. Suddenly she heard chachi shouting, 'Who called you here? Go, get out of this place.'

Maani had gone through a lot of suffering in life but this scolding pierced her heart like an arrow. She began to curse herself. *This is the reward you get for your childish behaviour. What was the need for you to come and join the married women?* Feeling small, she came out of the room and moved towards the staircase to go up and look for a place to cry alone in silence. Suddenly, on the staircase, she ran into Indranath, who was Gokul's classmate and best friend. He had also been invited for the wedding. He had come upstairs to look for Gokul. He had seen Maani a couple of times and knew that she was harshly treated in this household. He had also caught some of what chachi had said to Maani. He realized what was going on in Maani's mind as she climbed the stairs, so he followed her in order to console her, but the door was bolted from the inside. He peeped in through a crevice and saw Maani standing by a table and crying.

'Open the door, Maani,' he said softly.

Hearing his voice, Maani hid herself in a corner and asked, 'What is it?'

In a voice choked with emotion, Indranath said, 'Please open the door, I beg you.'

Such an appeal, soaked in affection, was an unprecedented experience for Maani. She had never imagined even in her dreams that in this cruel world anybody would implore her in this manner. Maani opened the door with trembling hands. Indranath charged into the room and saw a rope hanging from the ceiling fan. His heart shuddered. He immediately took out a knife from his pocket, cut the rope and said, 'What were you going to do, Maani? Do you know the punishment for this crime?'

Bowing her head, Maani said, 'Could there be a punishment worse than this? If a person whose face is despicable to people is punished harshly even when she dies, then there is no justice in the court of God. You do not know what my condition is like.'

Indranath's eyes became moist with tears. Maani had spoken nothing but the hard truth. He said, 'These days will not last forever, Maani. If you think there is nobody with you in this world, that is your illusion. There is at least one person who loves your life more than his own.'

Suddenly, Gokul was seen approaching. Maani rushed out of the room. Indranath's words had triggered something like a storm in her heart. What did he mean? She could not comprehend it at all. Yet, life seemed more meaningful to her today. A light had dawned in the darkness of her life.

3

Gokul was annoyed to see Indranath with Maani. His entire demeanour changed. After Maani left, he asked his friend harshly, 'When did you come here?'

Indranath responded in a steady manner, 'It was you I came here looking for. When I did not find you here, I was going to return downstairs. If I had gone, you would have found this door shut and a corpse hanging from the ceiling fan.'

Gokul surmised that Indranath was trying to make excuses to cover up his guilt. He said sharply, 'I never expected you to betray my confidence this way.'

Indranath's face turned red. He shot up and said, 'I did not expect you to slander me so badly either. I did not know that you considered me so depraved and crooked. Maani might be an object of contempt for you but she is and will always be an object of veneration for me. I do not have to give you any clarification for my conduct but Maani is much purer for me than you can ever understand. I do not want to raise these issues with you at this moment. I was looking for an appropriate time to say all this to you but I have to say it now because the occasion demands it. I knew that Maani was not respected in your house but that you consider her so depraved and disposable has only come to my notice now, after listening to your mother's comments. Your mother scolded her as one would spurn a dog just because she had gone to have a look at the bride's ornaments! You will say, "What could I do?" It is improper to drink water in a house where an orphan is tortured to such an extent. If you had made this clear to your mother in the beginning itself, things would not have come to such a pass. You cannot absolve yourself of this allegation. I cannot talk to your parents now because a wedding is being celebrated in your house but I have no hesitation in telling you that I would like to make Maani my life partner, and I would consider myself blessed if I did that. I had thought that I would first find a place to live and then make the proposal but I am afraid that a further delay in this matter might mean losing Maani. Therefore, to free you and your family from worries, I am making this proposal now.'

Gokul had never felt this kind of reverence for Indranath earlier. He was ashamed of himself for having suspected his friend. He also realized that in being indifferent to Maani for fear of his mother, he had ended up being a coward. It was an act of cowardice and nothing else. Sheepishly he said that if his mother had scolded Maani for no reason, it was a sign of her stupidity and that he would clarify this whenever he got a chance.

Indranath said, 'There is no time for inquiries and clarifications any more. I would like to talk to Maani and tell you what we decide. I do not want her to live here even for a moment longer. I have realized today that she is a self-respecting woman, and to tell you the truth, I am enamoured by her nature. Such a woman should not tolerate oppression.'

Gokul added hesitantly, 'But . . . do you know she is a widow?'

When we see someone being unusually generous to us, we unravel all our flaws to him. We want to show him that we are not entirely unworthy of his favour.

Indranath said with a smile, 'Yes, I know. I have heard about it and that is why I did not dare say anything to your father. Although not knowing would not have made any difference to my decision. Forget being a widow, even if Maani were an untouchable or worse than the worst, for me she is a jewel of a woman. We look for an experienced person when we want help with little things but when it comes to a companion in life's journey, we consider prior experience to be a defect. I am not the one to suppress the law. There is no school greater than the school of adversity. One can happily surrender one's life strings to a person who has graduated from this school. To me, being a widow is not a handicap—it is an asset.'

Gokul said, 'But what about the people in your home?'

Indranath said firmly, 'I do not consider my family so stupid that they would object to this proposal. If they do, I would like to keep my destiny under my control. My elders have many rights over me. In many situations, I consider their desire to be the ultimate law but I do not wish to be controlled by anyone when it comes to the pursuit of my soul's progress. I wish to enjoy the pride of being the architect of my own life.'

'And if Maani does not accept, then?' asked Gokul doubtfully.

Indranath found this doubt totally baseless. He said, 'You are talking like a child, Gokul. It is a given that Maani will not accept easily. She will get kicked around, snubbed and abused but will continue to stay in this very house. It is not easy to erase *sanskara* but we will have to persuade her. We will have to exorcize her accumulated impressions. I am not in favour of widows getting married again. I think the ideal of exclusive dedication to one's husband is the most priceless jewel on earth and we should attack it with care but this problem does not arise vis-à-vis Maani. Love and devotion are for a person and not to a name. She cannot be in love with a man she has not even seen. It is only a matter of ritual and convention. We should not worry about this display and outward show. I think somebody is calling you. I will also go now . . . I'll see you in a couple of days. But you don't hesitate and think too much about it, and let days go by.'

Gokul put his arms around Indranath and said, 'I will come to you myself day after tomorrow.'

4

The wedding party had departed. The guests had also left. It was nine o'clock It is well known how soundly one sleeps after a wedding! Everybody in the house had been asleep since the evening. Some slept on the charpoy, some on the wooden settee, some on the floor; one slept wherever one found space. Only Maani was taking care of the house, and Gokul was sitting in his room upstairs and reading the newspaper.

Suddenly, Gokul called out, 'Maani, get me a glass of cold water, please, I am very thirsty.'

Maani went upstairs with a glass of water and was about to leave after keeping it on the table when Gokul said, 'Just a minute, Maani, I have something to say to you.'

Maani replied, 'I have no time to talk, brother. The entire household is fast asleep. An intruder could sweep the whole house clean.'

Gokul said, 'Let them now. If I were you, I would join the thieves and help them steal. I am going to see Indranath just now. I have promised to see him today. Answer me quickly and please do not hesitate. He will get restless if I delay. Indranath loves you—do you know that?'

Maani turned her face away and said, 'Is that why you have called me here? I do not know anything.'

Gokul said, 'This only he knows or you know. He wants to marry you according to Vedic rites. Do you agree to the match?'

Maani looked down shyly. She could not answer.

Gokul reiterated, 'Dada and Amma have not been told, you know the reason why. They'd rather kill you through constant threats or burn you bit by bit than give

you permission to marry. It would humiliate them. Now
the decision rests with you. I think you should accept the
proposal. Indranath certainly loves you and he is a man of
flawless character and immense daring. He is totally fearless.
I will be truly delighted to see you happy in life.'

Maani was overwhelmed but still could not utter a
word.

Gokul was irritated now. 'Look, Maani, this is not the
time to be quiet, what are you thinking?'

Maani said in a quivering voice, 'Yes.'

Gokul felt light-hearted and smiled. Maani ran away,
embarrassed.

5

In the evening Gokul told his mother, 'Amma, there is a
celebration in Indranath's house today. His mother is worried
about coping with the housework alone. I said that I would
send Maani to help out. With your permission, I will drop
Maani there. She will return in a day or two.'

Maani appeared at that moment. Gokul cast a sideways
glance at her. Maani almost froze in embarrassment. She
could not find an escape route.

His mother said, 'Why do you ask for my permission?
Take her if she is willing to go.'

Gokul said, 'Go, get ready. You have to go to Indranath's
house.'

Maani objected, 'I am not feeling well. I will not go.'

Gokul's mother said, 'Why don't you go? You will not
have to dig a well there.'

Maani sat in the tonga in her white sari. Her heart was pounding and her eyes overflowed with tears. Her heart was sinking for some reason, as if she was going to drown herself in the river.

When the tonga had travelled a little distance, she told Gokul, 'Brother, I am feeling nervous, let's go back, I beseech you.'

Gokul said, 'You are crazy. Everybody is waiting for you there and you are asking me to turn back.'

'My heart says that something terrible is going to happen.'

'And my heart says that you are going to become a queen.'

'Why don't we wait for five or ten days? Tell them I am sick.'

'Don't talk like a crazy person.'

'People will make fun of us!'

'As far as auspicious occasions are concerned, I don't really care what anyone says.'

'Amma will not let you enter the house because of me. You will also get scolded.'

'I don't care about that. That is her habit.'

The tonga reached its destination. Indranath's mother was a progressive woman. She welcomed the bride and led her in.

6

It was twelve o'clock when Gokul left for home. On the one hand, he had the joy of having completed an auspicious task, but on the other, he was scared of facing his family when they saw no sign of Maani returning. He decided to disclose everything the moment he reached home. It was pointless to hide anything. He would have to tell them the truth sooner or later. So why not today?

With this decision, he entered the house.

Opening the door, his mother said, 'What were you up to till this late hour? Why didn't you bring her along? Who will do the dishes and clean the kitchen in the morning?'

Bowing his head, Gokul said, 'She may not come back now, Amma. Arrangements have been made for her stay in that house.'

Wide-eyed, his mother blurted out in surprise, 'What nonsense! How can she live there?'

'She is now married to Indranath.'

His mother felt as if she had fallen from the sky. She completely lost her senses and did not realize what ugly abuses she spouted on her own son—*kulangaar*, pimp, bastard and so on. Finally, Gokul could not contain himself. He lost his patience. His face turned red, his brows wrinkled. He said, 'Amma, that's enough. I don't have the patience to take this any more. If I had done anything improper I would not have raised my head even if you had beaten me with your slippers. But I have done nothing. I only did my duty, as any decent human being would do under the circumstances. You are a fool. You have no idea how times have changed. I have listened to your abuses with patience so far. You and, sadly enough, father, too, had made Maani's life a living hell. You treated her worse than one would treat an enemy. Just because she was dependent on you? Just because she was an orphan? She will not return to listen to your abuses any more. Hurt by your harsh words, she was going to commit suicide the day there was a wedding celebration in your house. If

Indranath had not reached there on time, we, you and the entire family, would have been sitting in jail today.'

Mother rolled her eyes and said ironically, 'Oh, what a great son you are—you saved the entire house from a disaster! And why not? This was your sister's turn. Next you will dispose *me* off to someone, so you can live in luxury. This is the best way to make your living. What was the use of getting an education?'

Gokul's heart ached and he writhed in agitation. In an anguished voice, he said, 'God forbid that a child be born from the womb of a mother like you. It's a sin to even look at your face.'

He left the house and walked away like a crazy man. A fierce wind was blowing but he felt as if there was no air for him to breathe.

7

A week went by but there was no sign of Gokul. Indranath had gone to Bombay, where he had found a place to live. After making arrangements for their stay, he wired his mother. Both she and Maani were to join him there. Vanshidhar had first suspected that Gokul might be hiding in Indranath's house. When he could not find him there he started looking for him everywhere in the city. All his visits to acquaintances, friends and relatives drew a blank. After running around the whole day, when he came back in the evening, he would take his wife to task saying, 'So, this is the result of cursing your son. Curse, curse, keep on cursing him again and again. God knows if you will ever come to your senses. The witch had left, you should have left the matter at that. Our burden had gone away. Keep a maidservant to manage the house. When she was not here, did we go hungry? Widows are getting married again, this is nothing unusual. If it were up to us, we would have thrown out the supporters of widow remarriage out of the country. We would have cursed them and burnt them alive but this is beyond our control. You too did not think it necessary to talk to me regarding this. I would have then done whatever I deemed fit. Did you think I would not come back from the office that day? That my last rites would be performed there? You just fell upon the boy! Now cry, cry as much as you can!'

Dusk had fallen. After scolding his wife Vanshidhar was walking restlessly outside his home. Time and again, he would get angry with Maani. *My home has been ruined because of this devil. God knows in what inauspicious moment she chose to come to us—she just ruined us! Had she not come here, we would not have witnessed these hard times. He was such a promising, talented lad, I wonder where he's gone!* Suddenly, an old woman walked up to him and said, 'Sir, I have this letter for you, please take it.'

Vanshidhar, his heart palpitating with hope, leapt forward and took the letter from the old woman. Perhaps Gokul had sent it. He could not decipher anything in the dark so he asked, 'Where did you get this from?'

The old woman replied, 'The wife of the gentleman who lives in Husainganj and is now working in Bombay has sent this letter.'

Vanshidhar went to the room, lit the lamp and started reading the letter. The letter was from Maani.

Respected Chachaji,

Accept pranams from the unfortunate Maani.

I was very sorry to hear that Gokul Bhaiya has gone somewhere and his whereabouts are not known. I am the cause. This stigma was meant for me and it has stuck. I am sorry that you had to suffer so much because of me. But bhaiya will definitely come back—I am sure about it. I am leaving for Bombay by the nine o'clock train tonight. Please forgive me for the offences I have committed and convey my pranams to chachi. My only prayer to God is that Gokul Bhaiya returns in good health. God willing I will visit you and pay my respects to you at bhaiya's wedding.

Vanshidhar tore the letter to pieces. He realized it was eight o'clock. Immediately, he changed his clothes, hired an ekka from the road and left for the station.

8

The Bombay Mail was waiting on the platform. There was a commotion among the passengers. The noisy call of the hawkers drowned out all other sounds. The train was about to leave. Maani and her mother-in-law were sitting in the ladies' compartment. Moist-eyed, Maani was looking out into the distance. Past memories, however unpleasant, can have a tinge of sweetness. Maani was remembering her earlier days of suffering and feeling happy that they were over. Who knows when she would meet Gokul again! If only chachaji had come she would have had a chance to pay her respects.

True, he had scolded her sometimes but it was always for her welfare. But he would not come. The train was about to leave. How could he come anyway? It would create a commotion in society. *God willing I shall see him when I come here next.*

Suddenly, she saw Vanshidhar approaching the train. She stepped out of the train and moved towards him. She was about to fall at his feet when he stepped back. Casting a wrathful glance at her, he said, 'Don't touch me, stay away, you . . . the unfortunate one. How dare you write to me after blackening your face! Why don't you die! You have ruined my clan. Till today we do not know where Gokul is. Because of you he left home and here you are still sitting on my chest, torturing me deliberately. Is there no water left in the Ganges for you to drown in? Had I realized that you were so unchaste and disloyal, I would have strangled you the very first day. Now you are trying to demonstrate your devotion to me! Sinners like you are better dead than alive. That would lighten the burden on this earth.'

A crowd of hundreds had gathered on the platform. Vanshidhar was hurling abuses at her mercilessly. No one understood what the matter was. But in their hearts all of them were condemning Vanshidhar.

Maani stood frozen like a statue. Her entire dignity lay shattered. She wished the earth would burst open and swallow her, that someone would strike her with a thunderbolt and put an end to her insignificant life! She had lost face in front of so many people. Not a drop of a tear fell from her eyes, for there were no tears left in her heart. There was a kind of burning forest fire instead which was fast engulfing her mind. Whose life could be more depraved than hers in this world?

Her mother-in-law called out, 'Bahu, get into the train.'

9

As the train moved, her mother-in-law said, 'I have never seen such a shameless person in my whole life. I am so enraged I wish I could have scratched his face.'

Maani did not raise her head.

Her mother-in-law said again, 'God knows when these wretched people will come to their senses, now it is almost time for them to die. Somebody should ask him —what can we do if his son has run away! Why would this calamity befall him if he were not such a sinner?'

Maani once again did not open her mouth. Perhaps she was unable to hear anything. Perhaps she was not even aware of her existence. She was fixedly gazing at the window—what was she perceiving in the dark?

The train arrived at Kanpur. Her mother-in-law said, 'Will you eat something, beti? Come, eat some sweets. It is past ten.'

Maani said, 'I am not hungry now, Amma. I will eat later.'

Her mother-in-law went to sleep. Maani also lay down but her uncle's face loomed large in front of her eyes and his words rang in her ears. 'Alas,' she moaned. 'I am so depraved, so low that the earth will be less burdened if I die.' She recalled Vanshidhar's words—Don't show your face again if you are your parents' daughter. I would not. If a face has been branded by slander, one does not feel like showing it to anyone.

The train moved on, piercing the heart of darkness. Maani opened her trunk and put away her ornaments. Then she took out Indranath's photograph and looked at it for a long time. Her eyes shone with a glint of pride. She put the photograph aside and said to herself, 'No, no, I cannot blot your life. You are godlike, you have taken pity on me. I am atoning for the sins of my past. You picked me up and pressed me close to your heart and I will not taint you. You love me and you will tolerate disrespect, insult and slander for me, but I will not be a burden on your life.'

The train chugged on. Maani kept gazing at the stars till they disappeared. She saw her mother's face in the dark so bright, so vivid that she closed her eyes with a start. Then she looked inside the compartment to see her mother-in-law sleeping.

10

God knows how much of the night had passed. Maani's mother-in-law woke up at the sound of the door opening. The train was moving very fast but there was no sign of her bahu. She rubbed her eyes, sat up and called out, 'Bahu, bahu.' But there was no reply.

Her heart started beating very fast. She cast a glance at the upper berth, looked inside the toilet, below the benches—bahu was nowhere. Then she stood at the doorway. She got suspicious—who had opened this door? Had someone come in? Her heart grew restless. She shut the door and started crying loudly. Who could she ask? The mail train would not stop for a while. *I had told her—Bahu, let's sit in the male compartment but she did not listen to me. She said, 'Amma, you will have trouble sleeping in a male compartment.' Now is this the comfort she has given me?*

Suddenly she remembered the alarm chain. She pulled the chain vigorously many times. The train stopped after several minutes. The guard arrived. A few more passengers joined in from the next compartment. They searched the entire compartment. They checked the boards below carefully. There was no trace of blood. They checked the luggage. Bedroll, box, small box, utensils—everything was there. All locks were intact. Nothing was missing. If someone had entered the compartment from outside where could he have gone from a moving train? It was impossible to jump from a train carrying a woman. From these signs, all those present concluded that Maani must have fallen down after losing her grip on the handlebar. The guard was a nice fellow. He got off the train and searched for Maani for one mile on both sides of the railway track. There was no trace of her. What more could be done at night beyond that! Some people insisted upon taking Mataji to the men's compartment. It was decided that Mataji should get off the train at the next station and a full search operation be carried out in the morning.

We start depending on others in times of adversity. Mataji looked around for help here and there. Her plaintive eyes seemed to be saying—*Why can't someone bring back my daughter? Oh, she had barely tasted marital joy, she was so excited about going to her husband! Someone should go to that wicked Vanshidhar and tell him, 'Look, your desire has been fulfilled. Are you happy now?*

The old woman sat crying and the train kept moving, breaking through the darkness.

11

It was Sunday evening. Indranath was sitting on the terrace with a couple of friends. There was fun and laughter all around as Maani's arrival was awaited. A friend said, 'Why, Indra, you have some experience of married life, what do you advise us? Shall we build a nest somewhere or shall we spend the rest of our lives sitting on the branches? From journals and magazines it seems that there is little difference between married life and hell.'

Indranath smiled and said, 'This is a matter of destiny, absolutely a stroke of luck. If married life is like hell on the one hand, it is no less than heaven on the other.'

Another friend said, 'Will there be this kind of freedom?'

Indranath said, 'Not even one per cent of this. If you wish to return from a movie at midnight, to wake up at nine o'clock. and play cards after returning from office at four, then marriage will not bring you any happiness. If you can get a suit stitched every month now, then you may not even get one in a year.'

'Your respected spouse is coming by train tonight, isn't she?'

'Yes, by mail train. Why don't you come to the station to receive her?'

'You don't have to ask me. Why go home now? But you will have to treat us to dinner tomorrow.'

Suddenly, the postman came and handed Indranath an envelope.

Indranath's face lit up. He slit open the envelope and started reading it at once. As soon as he read it, his heart was paralysed, his breathing stopped and his head reeled. He lost his vision, as though a black curtain had enveloped the earth. He flung the telegram to his friends and started crying bitterly, his face covered with both his hands. Perturbed, his friends picked up the telegram nervously and looked at the wall.

They recalled what they had been looking forward to and look what had happened!

The telegram read like this:

Maani jumped off the train. Her corpse was discovered three miles from Laalpur. I am in Laalpur. Come immediately.

One of the friends said, 'An enemy might have sent a false report.'

The second friend said, 'Yes, sometimes people indulge in such mischief.'

Indranath looked at them blankly but said nothing.

For many minutes, all three sat quiet and motionless. Suddenly, Indranath stood up and said, 'I shall leave by this very train.'

The train was to leave Bombay at nine. Both friends quickly wrapped the bedroll and got it ready. One picked up the bedroll and the other, the box. Indranath hurriedly changed his clothes and left for the station. Despair led and hope followed.

12

One week had passed. Vanshidhar had just arrived home from office when Indranath came and offered his respects. Vanshidhar was startled to see him, not at his unexpected arrival but at his dishevelled appearance.

Vanshidhar asked, 'You had gone to Bombay, no?'

Indranath said, 'Yes, I have only just come back.'

Vanshidhar said in a sharp tone, 'You destroyed Gokul.'

Indranath looked at his ring and said, 'He is at my place.'

Vanshidhar's sad face lit up. He said, 'Why didn't he come here? Where did you meet Gokul? Had he gone to Bombay?'

'No, I met him at the railway station yesterday when I got off the train.'

'Then go get him. Let bygones be bygones.'

Saying this, Indranath ran towards the house. In a minute, Gokul's mother called him indoors.

Gokul's mother looked at him from head to toe and said, 'Were you sick, bhaiya? Why do you look so crestfallen?'

Gokul's mother gave him a *lota* full of water and said, 'Wash your hands and face, son. Gokul is all right, I suppose? Where were you all these days? How many times I have prayed for his return! Why has he not come?'

Indranath said, washing his hands and face, 'I did suggest that he should come but he didn't out of fear.'

'Where was he all these days?'

'He said he was roaming around in the villages.'

'So, you have come alone from Bombay?'

'Not really, Amma has also come with me.'

Gokul's mother asked with some hesitation, 'Maani is in a good place, isn't she?'

Indranath smiled and said, 'Yes, she is in great bliss now. She is free from all earthly bonds.'

His mother said in disbelief, 'Don't be naughty now. Are you cursing the poor girl? But tell me, why have you come back from Bombay so soon?'

Indranath said with a smile again, 'What could I do? I got a telegram from Mataji saying that Maani had jumped off the train and ended her life. Her body was lying in Laalpur. I rushed there. That's where I performed the cremation and other rites. I returned home only today. Please forgive my offence now.'

He could say no more. Tears welled up and choked his throat. He took out a letter from his pocket and kept it in front of her and said, 'I found only this letter in her box.'

For a long time, Gokul's mother sat in speechless anguish, gazing at the floor. Grief and more aptly repentance had overpowered her senses. She picked up the letter and started reading it.

Swami!

When you get this letter in your hands, I will be gone from this world. I am very unfortunate. I have no place in this world. Because of me, you too will be in trouble and be condemned. I thought about it and decided that it is best for me to die. How do I reciprocate the compassion you have showered on me? I had never desired anything in life but I regret not dying at your feet. My last request to you is that you do not mourn for me. May God always keep you happy.

'She' kept the letter aside and tears started flowing from her eyes. Vanshidhar stood in the veranda motionless, as if Maani stood before him, in all her modesty.

Translated from the Hindi by Neerja M. Chand

The Widow with Sons

1

When Pandit Ayodhyanath passed away, everyone remarked, 'May God give such an end to everyone!'

He was survived by four grown-up sons, all married, and a daughter, yet unmarried. He had left behind a considerable fortune; a brick-house, two orchards, jewellery worth several thousands of rupees, and twenty thousand in hard cash. For a long time, Phulmati, his widow, remained in a state of mourning, but she composed herself with the thought that she had four grown-up sons to look to. All four of them were impeccably mannered and all their wives exceedingly obedient. When she lay down at night, the four of them took turns to massage her feet. When she would take her bath it is they who picked out a sari for her. Thus the entire household danced to her tune. The eldest son, Kamatanath, worked in an office for fifty rupees a month. Umanath, the younger one, had qualified as a doctor and was hoping to open up a clinic. The third, Dayanath, having failed his BA examination, was somehow managing a living by writing for magazines. Sitanath, the fourth, was the brightest of them all, and having passed his BA in the first division, was now preparing for his MA examination. None of the sons had any vices, or had such improvident habits that would bring grief to the mother or disgrace the family honour. For all practical purposes, Phulmati was in charge of the household. However, the keys remained in the custody of the eldest bahu. The old woman did not make an ostentatious show of her authority which often makes the elderly irascible and querulous, but no one could demand and have anything without her wish.

It was evening. Twelve days had gone by since Panditji had passed away. Tomorrow would be the thirteenth day of the death rites. A big ritual feast to which all relatives and members of the fraternity were invited, had to be arranged. The preparations were in progress. Phulmati, seated in her room, could see people bringing in bagful of flour, ghee tins, baskets full of vegetables, bags of sugar and containers of curd. Several other things were brought for offering; utensils, clothes, beds, bedding, umbrellas, shoes, sticks and lanterns, but Phulmati was not shown anything. As had been the custom, all these items should have been first brought to her for approval. She would size everything up, approve of it, and would suggest proper measure, before it could be stored. But, why was she not consulted, or shown anything? And why only three bags of flour when she had asked for five. Ghee too was only in five tins when she had asked for ten. Similarly, every other item like vegetables, sugar, curds must have been cut down upon. Who dared to interfere with her orders? Once she had decided on something, who could have any right to tamper with the quantities?

For forty years, Phulmati's word prevailed in all matters. If she wished hundred rupees to be spent, hundred were spent; if she asked for one, then just one. Nobody ever did any nitpicking. Even Pandit Ayodhyanath didn't ever go against her wishes. But, today, right in front of her eyes, she was being ignored. How could she tolerate all this?

For a moment, she kept quiet; but couldn't restrain herself any longer. She was used to her rightful autonomy. Full of anger, she went to Kamatanath and said, 'Why have you brought just three bags of flour; I had asked for five? And ghee, too, is only in five tins. Don't you remember I had asked for ten? Prudence is not bad but if a person who dug the well himself remained thirsty—isn't that such a disgrace?'

Kamatanath did not care to say he was sorry, nor did he feel ashamed. For a moment he stood defiant, then said, 'We decided on three bags for which five tins of ghee would be enough. In the same way we cut down on the other quantities too.'

Phulmati reacted sharply, 'Who suggested a cut in the flour?'

'We did.'

'Does my opinion count for nothing?'

'Why not, but we too can understand our gain and loss.'

A flabbergasted Phulmati stared at him. She couldn't get what he intended by 'gain and loss'. She very well understood the gain and the loss of this household. Others, even if born of her, had no business to interfere with what she did. This insolent fellow was talking back as if the house belonged to him alone, as if he had suffered to raise this family, and she was an outsider. Look at his audacity!

Her face flushed with anger as she retorted, 'You are not to count my gain or loss. I have the right to do what I think proper. Go right away and bring two more bags of flour and five tins of ghee, and beware of disregarding my orders in future.'

She had given him quite a dressing-down. Perhaps she shouldn't have been so harsh. She felt sorry for it. Well, they were boys after all. It was natural for them to think in terms of economy. Maybe they didn't ask me because they knew I myself am thrifty. Had they known that I wouldn't skimp on anything in this matter, they wouldn't have dared defy me. Although Kamatanath was standing in the same manner, it was apparent that he was in no mood to comply. Phulmati, however, felt assured, and went off to her room. She couldn't have entertained the thought of someone not following her word.

As time passed by, it became apparent to her that she no longer had the same status in this house that she had enjoyed ten or twelve days ago. From the kinsmen came various offerings of sugar, sweetmeats, curds, pickle, etc., which were stowed away by the eldest bahu as her own possessions. No one came around to take her advice. If any of the relatives had something to ask, they went straight to Kamatanath or his wife, as if he was the most responsible or resourceful person of the house. In fact, most of the time he could be found stoned with bhang. Somehow he managed to go to his office, but that too, for no more than fifteen days in a month. The sahibs had regard for Panditji or else he would have been fired long ago. His wife, an insensitive woman, could not appreciate a situation like this. She was not even capable of taking care of her personal belongings, let alone manage the household. What a shame! They were all bent upon bringing disgrace to the family. At some stage, something or the other could run out of stock. One needs to exercise a lot of prudence to see to such things. Something may be in surplus and one wouldn't know how to dispose it of, while other items would be in such small quantities that they would hardly reach each platter. What has struck all of them? Well, why was the eldest bahu opening the safe? Who is she to do that without my permission? The keys are in her custody, all right, but she is not supposed to open the safe unless I authorize her to do so. But look at her, today she is opening the safe as if I count for nothing. No, I can't stand it any more.

Rising peremptorily she went over to the eldest bahu and said sternly, 'Why are you opening the safe? I never asked you to!'

The elder bahu replied nonchalantly, 'Won't we pay for the things purchased?'

'I don't know anything about how things were purchased and in what quantities? How can there be payments unless there are proper accounts?'

'Well, all is settled.'

'Who did that?'

'How do I know? Go and ask the men. I was ordered to fetch money for payments, and I am merely doing that.'

Phulmati could hardly suppress her ire. But it was no time to get into a foul mood. The house was full of guests— men, women, all. If she lost her temper with the boys now, the people will gossip that the family was splitting up soon after Panditji had died. She braced herself and walked up and withdrew to her room. But she was determined to take everyone to task once the guests had left. Let her see how they face her and respond to her. She was going to smash the coterie.

She felt restless even in her room and kept an eagle-eyed watch on the entire scene. Which rules of hospitality were not observed? Where had someone overstepped the bounds of honour? The feast had begun. All the guests were asked to be seated in rows. The courtyard had room for barely two hundred people. She wondered how five hundred people could be accommodated in this space. Were they going to pile up one upon the other? Would there be two shifts? What was the harm if the people were to be seated in two shifts? At the most, the feast would be over by two at night rather than at twelve. But everybody seems to be in a hurry to get away and sleep. Let this damn thing be over so that one may sleep in peace. The diners are sitting so close to one another that one can't even move edgeways. The *pattals* are overlapping. The puris served have gone cold—there is a clamour for hot puris. When the *maida* puris become cold, they stiffen like leather. Who is going to eat such stuff! Why has the cook been sent off so early? So very irritating!

Suddenly, there was an uproar. The vegetable dishes had no salt. The elder bahu quietly set about powdering salt. Enraged, Phulmati was biting her lips, but couldn't have spoken at such a juncture. At last salt powder was brought and sprinkled over the platters. There was another uproar: 'The water is hot—we need cold water.' But cold water had not been arranged for; no one had thought of getting any ice. Someone was rushed to the market but where could one get ice so late in the night? The fellow returned empty-handed. Guests had to make do with the warm tap water. If Phulmati had her way, she would tear the boys from limb to limb. Her house had never before witnessed such ignominy. And yet, everyone was dying to be the master of the house. It hadn't occurred to anyone to order for such an essential item as ice. How would it strike anyone when they were busy gossiping? How must the guests be wondering there wasn't any ice in the house and the entire community had been invited to a feast?

There was more commotion. The diners were getting up from their places. What must the matter be?

Phulmati could not remain unconcerned. Emerging from her room she came into the courtyard and asked Kamatanath, 'What is the matter, son? Why are the people getting up?'

Kamatanath did not answer her, and quietly slipped away from there. That irritated Phulmati. Suddenly she met the maid and asked her the same question. She was told that a dead mouse was found in someone's curry. Phulmati stood transfixed. She was in a terrible rage, fuming from within, as if she would dash out her brains against the wall. These accursed fellows were in charge of the feast. It was the height of grossness. How many people have had their dharma abused. Why won't they get up after witnessing all this? Everything has come to nought. Hundreds of rupees have gone to waste; not to talk of this utter ignominy.

The guests have dispersed. And the food was still lying on the pattals. All four sons standing in the courtyard were a picture of disgrace. They were now blaming each other. The eldest bahu was getting angry at the younger ones, who in turn put all the blame on Kumud, which made her cry. Just then, Phulmati appeared and burst out: 'Are you satisfied with the disgrace you have brought on or is there something still left? Go and drown yourself, all of you. We cannot show our faces in the town.'

None of the sons responded.

Phulmati became more vehement: 'It doesn't affect you, since none of you has any sense of honour. Only he who has spent his life bringing dignity to this house can grieve. Why have you brought disrepute to his noble soul? The entire community has contempt for us. No one will ever come to even urinate at your door.'

Kamatanath listened to her silently for a while, then got irritated and said, 'Now keep quiet, Amma. We admit our mistake, indeed, this was a blunder. But are you going to hang us for this? Everyone commits mistakes only to repent later. But you do not cry for their blood.'

The eldest bahu tried to clear it up. 'How would we know Kumud couldn't do even this much of the job? She should have checked the vegetables before pouring them into the cauldron. She just emptied the whole basket into it. How can we be blamed for this?'

Kamatanath admonished his wife, 'No single person, not even Kumud, not you, nor I is to blame for this. It was just a matter of chance. We were destined for this disgrace. When there is such a big feast, you do not put fistfuls of vegetables into the *karhai*. Entire baskets have to be emptied. Such mishaps do take place occasionally.

'How can this be an object of mockery or disgrace? You are unnecessarily adding insult to injury.'

Phulmati gnashed her teeth in disgust and said, 'Instead of feeling ashamed, you speak so insolently.'

Kamatanath was not one to be subdued. 'Why should I be ashamed? Have I committed some theft? Ants in sugar and pests in wheat are easily overlooked. We didn't watch out and that was a slip—that was it. Or else we would have quietly thrown out the mouse and none would be any the wiser.'

Phulmati was aghast at hearing this. 'What did you say? The dead mouse would have defiled everyone's dharma.'

Kamata said smilingly, 'Amma, which age are you living in? Such trifles do not corrupt anyone's dharma. Tell me who among the so-called virtuous people who walked off from there don't eat meat? They won't spare even tortoises and snails. How would a little mouse defile them?'

Phulmati felt as if doomsday was very near. 'God save dharma! Even educated people harbour such unrighteous notions.' Cut up, she withdrew.

2

Two months went by. Night had fallen. The four brothers, having done with the day's work or jobs were sitting in the room and chatting. The eldest bahu was in league with them, the topic being discussed was Kumud's wedding.

Kamatanath reclined against the bolster and said, 'Father's words are gone with him. Pandit Murari is a learned man and should be a gentleman. But a person who barters his learning and status for money is rather mean and we couldn't marry Kumud off to such a person's son, not for an amount, let alone a dowry of five thousand rupees. Send him a refusal and look out for another groom. We only have twenty thousand rupees with us, which means five thousand as each one's share. If we set aside five thousand for dowry and five thousand for other things, such as band, etc., we will be stripped of all the money we have.'

Umanath quipped, 'I need at least five thousand rupees to start my clinic. I cannot spare anything out of my share.

In the beginning, there will be hardly any earnings and I shall have to fall back on whatever resources I have.'

Dayanath was looking at a newspaper. Taking off his glasses, he said, 'I too, am thinking of publishing a newspaper. I need a capital of at least ten thousand rupees for the printing press and the newspaper. If I can invest five thousand rupees, somebody can chip in as a partner with another five thousand rupees. I can't get by on writing articles for others' newspapers.'

Kamatanath nodded in agreement. 'No one publishes articles even for free, let alone pays for them.'

Dayanath contradicted him and said, 'Well, not really. I don't write for anyone unless I get some advance.'

Kamatanath took his words back. 'I am not speaking of you, you may be getting paid, but not everyone can manage that.'

The elder bahu said, 'If a girl is born under lucky stars she will be happy even in an impoverished home. But if she is unlucky, she will feel miserable even in a king's home. It is all a matter of destiny.'

Kamatanath looked at his wife with admiration. 'We have to marry Sita off this very year.'

Sitanath was the youngest of the brothers. Even while keeping his head down, he was getting impatient to criticize the selfish motives of his brothers. So as soon as he heard his name, he said, 'Do not bother about my marriage. I will not even talk of it unless I start earning. Truly speaking, I don't really want to marry. What our country needs is people who work, rather than adding to the population. You can spend my share of the money on Kumud's wedding. Having once fixed with Pandit Murarilal, it would be unbecoming to snap the relations.'

Uma protested loudly. 'How do we manage ten thousand rupees?'

Sita said with some diffidence, 'I am willing to contribute my share of the money.'

'What about the remaining amount?'

'Murarilal can be asked to lower the dowry demand. He cannot be so selfish as not to be accommodating. If he is satisfied with three thousand rupees, the marriage can be arranged within five thousand rupees.'

Uma said to Kamatanath, 'Do you hear what he is saying?'

Dayanath spoke up, 'What is the harm? He is giving up his share, why not spend it? We have no grudge against Murari Pandit. On the other hand, I am happy to know that there is someone among us who is willing to make a sacrifice. He has no immediate need for money. He gets a stipend from the government. As soon as he passes his examination he will find some job. We are not that lucky.'

Kamatanath spoke with circumspection, 'What would he know about loss? If one of us suffers should others do something about it? He hasn't yet grown up and doesn't realize that a single rupee is worth a lakh of rupees in difficult circumstances. Who knows he might get a scholarship to study in a foreign country, or get selected for the civil services. At that time he will require at least four to five thousand rupees to equip himself with. Where will he then go begging for money? I don't want him to ruin his life for the sake of a dowry for Kumud.'

Sitanath couldn't refute his argument. With some hesitation he conceded, 'In that case, I shall need the money.'

'Is that not likely to happen?'

'It is not unlikely, but perhaps difficult. Those who can manage recommendations get scholarships. Who is going to bother about me?'

'At times recommendations count for nothing and those without them romp home.'

'Well, do as you wish. As far as I am concerned I can forgo an overseas trip, but want Kumud married off into a good family.'

'You don't get a family only with a dowry. As your *bhabhi* said, it is all in one's stars. What I want is that Murarilal should be sent a refusal and we should look for a groom who would agree to a small dowry. I cannot afford to spend more than a thousand rupees on this marriage. How about Pandit Deendayal?'

Uma was delighted to hear that and said, 'He is excellent. Doesn't matter if he is not an MA and BA, but he earns a good living from his *jajmani*.'

Dayanath objected, 'We should seek Amma's opinion.'

But Kamatanath saw no need for this, and said, 'She has lost her reason, and has the same orthodox views. She is all out for Murarilal. Doesn't realize that the times have changed. All she wants is to send Kumud to Murari's house, even if we are ruined in the bargain.'

Uma expressed some doubt. 'You just watch out, Amma is going to give away all her jewellery to Kumud.'

Kamatanath couldn't be so selfish. 'Well, the jewellery is her sole possession. It is her dower. She can give it to anyone she likes.'

Uma interjected, 'It is her dower, but does that mean she should squander it away? After all, that too was Dada's earning?'

'Whosoever might have earned it, but she has full rights on it.'

'These are labyrinths of law. Twenty thousand will have four claimants and jewellery worth ten thousand will be only Amma's. You just wait and watch; she will marry Kumud off to Murari Pandit on the strength of this jewellery.'

Umanath was in no mind to let go of such a huge amount. He was adept at trickery. He would cook up some story and wangle the jewels out of the mother. Till then it would be rather indiscreet to provoke Phulmati by bringing up the subject of Kumud's marriage. Umanath nodded his head and said, 'The jewellery will be of no less value than ten thousand rupees.'

Kamatanath was not moved and said, 'Whatever their worth, I cannot be party to something that is unethical.'

'All right then, you be off. Don't jump in later to upset things.'

'I'll stay away from all this.'

'And you, Sita?'

'I too will stay away.'

But when Dayanath was told about it, he promptly agreed to conspire with him.

He will at least get two and a half out of ten. If one has to resort to some trickery for such a large sum, it's all in the game.

3

Phulmati had retired after her dinner when Uma and Daya came over to her. They looked so pathetic in appearance as if some great calamity had befallen them. Phulmati asked apprehensively, 'Both of you look perturbed.'

Uma scratched his head and said, 'Writing for newspapers is a risky business, Amma. However cautious you may be, you get caught sometime or the other. Dayanath wrote an article for which a surety of five thousand rupees has been demanded from him. If the amount is not deposited by tomorrow, he will be arrested and sent to jail for ten years.'

Phulmati beat her head in desperation. 'Why do you write such things, son, you should know we are already passing through tough times? Can't the surety be avoided?'

Dayanath replied sheepishly, 'Amma, I had not written any such thing, but what to do about misfortune? The district magistrate is so strict that he will show no mercy. I have left no stone unturned.'

'In that case didn't you ask Kamata to arrange the money?'

Uma said with a grimace, 'You know his nature, Amma, money is dearer to him than life. He may be condemned to solitary confinement, but he will not part with a single pie.'

Dayanath supported him. 'I didn't think it proper to even take this issue to him.'

Phulmati, rising from her bed, said, 'Come with me, I will tell him, how can he refuse to give? Money is meant for such emergencies and not to be kept hidden underground.'

Umanath stopped his mother and said, 'Amma, don't tell him anything. Instead of giving money he will raise hell. He is more concerned with saving his own job, and he won't even allow Dayanath to live in the house. I wouldn't be surprised if he even reports it to the officers.'

Phulmati felt helpless. 'So how are you going to arrange for the surety? I have got nothing with me. Yes, I do have my jewellery. Take these and pawn them with someone to deposit the surety amount. And swear that you will never write such things for any newspaper.'

Dayanath put his hands on his ears. 'Amma, it is just not possible for me to take away your jewellery to save my skin. No matter if I am sentenced to ten or five years' imprisonment. I shall go through this ordeal. What purpose do I serve here?'

Phulmati, beating her breast, said, 'What are you saying, my son—who has the guts to arrest you as long as I am alive? Won't I torch his face? Isn't the jewellery meant for such a rainy day? What shall I do with it if you are not around? Throw it into the fire?'

She brought out the jewellery box and put it in front of him.

Daya looked at Uma beseechingly, and said, 'What is your opinion, Bhai Sahib? That is the reason I was telling you there was no need to tell Amma about it. The worst that can happen is that I will end up in jail.'

Uma as if coming to his defence said, 'How is it that such a calamity would have passed Amma by? It wasn't possible for me to keep quiet about it. I just can't see what is to be done now. I don't want you to go to jail nor is it right to pawn Amma's jewellery.'

Phulmati said in a plaintive voice, 'Do you think the jewellery is dearer to me than you are? I can even sacrifice my life for your sake, the jewellery is not even worth mentioning.'

Daya said resolutely, 'Amma, I won't have your jewellery whatever misfortune may befall me. I have been of no use to you so far, how can I now take away your jewellery? A wicked son like me should not have been born to you. I have always given you pain.'

Phulmati spoke up as firmly, 'If you do not accept these jewels I will myself go and pawn these and shall deposit the amount with the district magistrate. You can test me if you like. God alone knows what will happen when I am no more, but as long as I am alive, nobody can ever touch you.'

Umanath, as if obliging his mother, said, 'There is no other way left for us now. There is no harm, then, accept these, but remember to redeem and return the jewellery as soon as you have the money. It is true that motherhood is a long process of sacrifice. Who else but a mother can shower so much love? We are so unfortunate that we do not show even a fraction of the respect which is due to her.'

Both of them, as if getting over a big dilemma, took charge of the jewellery box and took off. Their mother looked at them lovingly as if all her being's blessings were eager to embrace them. Today, after so many months her heart, shadowed with grief, got some solace after making this sacrifice of all she had. Her whole being was indeed looking for ways and means to surrender her possessions. Her attitude never smacked of greed or self-interest. She knew that her enjoyment and her authority lay in sacrifice. She felt overwhelmed as if her rights had been restored to her.

4

Three more months passed. After making away with their mother's jewellery all four brothers began fawning upon her. They also instructed their wives not to give her any offence. If being a little polite could placate her heart, what was the harm in it? They did what pleased them but took care to take her token advice. They manipulated things in such a manner that she would be easily taken in by them to give her ready consent. She was most unwilling to sell the orchard but they cooked up such stories that she felt compelled to consent to the sale. However, no consensus could be reached regarding Kumud's marriage. The mother was intent on Pandit Murarilal whereas the sons were bent upon Deendayal. Then they quarrelled over the matter one day.

Phulmati declared that a daughter, too, had all the claims on her parents' money. She told the sons, 'You got the orchards worth sixteen thousand rupees and a house worth twenty-five thousand rupees. Can't she claim even five thousand out of the cash of twenty thousand?'

Kamata said politely, 'Amma, Kumud is not only your daughter, she is our sister, too. You will pass away in two to four years but our relation with her will last long years. We will never do anything that goes against her well-being, but as far as a share for her is concerned she is entitled to nothing whatsoever. It was different when Dada was alive. He could have spent as much as he liked on her marriage. No one would have restrained him, but things are different now. We have to manage everything with utmost care and look after every paisa. There is no wisdom in blowing five thousand if something can be managed within one thousand.'

Umanath corrected him, 'Not five thousand, but ten thousand.'

Kamata shrugged it off and said, 'No, I will say five thousand. It is not within our means to spend five thousand rupees.'

Phulmati put her foot down. 'Come what may, she will be married off only to Murarilal's son, no matter five thousand

or ten thousand. After all, it is all my husband's earning. I
have put it together with great difficulty. And I will spend it
as I like. You alone are not born of me. Kumud too has taken
birth from the same womb. All of you are equal in my eyes.
I am not begging anything of anyone. You just sit and watch
the show, I will manage everything. Out of twenty thousand
rupees, five thousand belong to Kumud.'

Kamatanath was left with no choice but to speak out
the bitter truth, and said, 'Amma, you are unnecessarily
aggravating the situation. The money that you think is
yours doesn't really belong to you but to us. You can't spend
anything out of it without our permission.'

Phulmati felt as if she had been bitten by a snake. 'What
did you say? Come on, repeat it. I can't spend my own
money?'

'The money is not yours, it belongs to us.'

'Yours only after my death.'

'Not so, it became ours as soon as Dada died.'

Umanath said shamelessly, 'Amma doesn't understand
the law and quarrels with us unnecessarily.'

Phulmati spoke in anger and indignation, 'To hell with
your law. I don't respect such law. Your father was not a
millionaire. I scrimped and saved and held the family together
or you would have no shelter for yourself. You can't touch my
money as long as I am alive. I spent ten thousand rupees on
each of your brothers' weddings, and I am going to spend the
same amount on Kumud's marriage.'

Kamatanath grew wild. 'You have no right to spend
anything.'

Umanath admonished his elder brother, 'Bhai sahib, you
are unnecessarily arguing with Amma. Simply write a letter to

Murarilal telling him that Kumud can't be married into their family. That's the end of it. She doesn't understand any law and gets into useless arguments.'

Phulmati composed herself and said, 'Well, let me hear what the law says.'

Uma said with exasperation, 'The law says that the ancestral property goes to the sons after their father's death. The mother is merely entitled to food and clothes.'

Phulmati reacted sharply. 'Who made this law?'

Uma said quietly, 'Our rishis, the maharaja Manu, who else?'

For a moment Phulmati was dumbstruck and then let out painfully, 'So, I am living in this house at your mercy.'

Umanath said impassively, 'Well, you may take it as you like.'

Phulmati cried out at this thunderbolt. The words emitted as sparks as she said, 'I made the house; I managed the property, I gave you birth and brought you up. And today I am a stranger in my own house? Is that Manu's edict, and do you want to follow it? All right, have your house to yourself. I can't go on living here as your dependant. I would rather die. What a shock! I planted the tree but can't stand in its shade. If that is the law, to hell with it!'

The four youngsters were not in the least intimidated by this show of anger of their mother. As they thought they had the protective shield of law, how could such pinpricks harm them?

After a short while, Phulmati left. For the first time, she felt that her disheartened motherhood was cursing her. The motherhood, her sole treasure, which she had cherished above all her aspirations, was now a burning furnace, into the flames of which her life was consigned.

It was evening. The neem tree in the courtyard stood with drooping branches as if depressed with the ways of the world. On the western horizon the lord of light and life was burning it its own pyre; so was Phulmati's motherhood.

5

When Phulmati retired to her room and lay on the bed, she felt as if her back was broken. Even in her dreams it had never occurred to her that her own sons would turn into her enemies as soon as her husband died. The sons whom she had nurtured and suckled were inflicting terrible wounds on her heart. This house was now a bed of thorns for her.

To live here and feed herself in a place where she had lost all respect and counted for nothing was something that was unbearable to her proud nature.

But what was the way out for her? If she lived apart from the sons who was going to suffer the disgrace? Whether the world cursed her or cursed her sons, it was all the same, she was the one who would be held responsible for the indignity. The people would gossip that with four young sons around, the old woman lived separately and had to labour for her meals. Those whom she always considered below her status will laugh at her. No, such humiliation would be more heart-rending than this disregard. It was wiser to keep her own and her family's honour under wraps. She would now have to adapt herself to new circumstances. Times had changed. So far she had been in command, but now she was compelled to live like a servant. This was the will of God. It would be better to suffer the jibes and blows of her own sons rather than those of outsiders.

She covered her face and wept over her wretched plight. The long night passed in this suffering. The winter dawn emerged from the darkness, full of trepidation, as if coming out of jail. Much against her habit, Phulmati got up very early that morning. It appeared as if she had undergone a mental metamorphosis during the course of the night. While the entire household slept, she began to sweep the courtyard. The ground hardened by the midnight frost stung her bare feet like thorns. Panditji would have never allowed her to wake up so early. The cold was very harmful for her. But those days were gone. She was trying to adjust herself to the times. Having done the sweeping, she lit some fire and began to pick pebbles off the rice and lentils. After some time, the sons woke up, but no one said to her, 'Amma, why are you bothering yourself with all this work?' They were probably happy that the proud spirit of the old woman was crushed.

From then onwards, Phulmati was determined to work with all her might, but with complete indifference. In place of the proud, self-confident expression on her face, there was deep anguish. In place of the bright electric light, there was a timorous lamp, which would be snuffed out with the slightest whiff of a gentle wind.

Finally, it was decided that a letter of refusal would be sent to Murarilal. The very next day, the letter was written. Kumud's wedding was settled with Deendayal who, over forty years old, didn't have much of a social standing, and barely earned his livelihood. He expressed no reservations and readily agreed to marry Kumud. The wedding day was fixed, the *baraat* came, the wedding ceremony took place and Kumud was sent off.

Nobody knew how Phulmati felt. But all four brothers were happy as if a thorn had been removed from their flesh. As for Kumud, how could a high-born daughter open her mouth? She would either enjoy her life or live in sorrow, depending on what luck had in store for her. One is always helpless and has to submit to God's will. If the family elders selected her life partner, he had to be looked up to with devotion, no matter what his failings may be. He was her lord. There was no question of resisting what had been allotted to her.

Phulmati did not intervene in anything, whether it concerned gifts for Kumud, or entertaining the guests, or the money or gifts received from the invitees—she was not concerned with anything. Even if someone came to take her advice, her response was, 'Whatever you do is fair enough, my sons, why ask me?'

When the *doli* for Kumud arrived at the gate, she embraced her mother and started crying. Phulmati took her daughter to her room and whatever was left in her possession, hundred or fifty odd rupees and some jewels, she put all into her lap and said, 'Beti, all my desires are smothered within me; or else you wouldn't be married and be sent off in this way.'

Phulmati had never talked about her jewellery to anyone so far. She may not have realized how her sons had duped her but she knew she wouldn't get her jewellery back. Speaking of it now would be of no avail, and would only breed rancour. However, she wanted to make things clear on this occasion. The thought that Kumud would go away with the impression that Amma had saved her jewellery for her bahus instead of giving it to her, would be unbearable to her. That was the reason she had taken Kumud to her room, but Kumud had already sensed the treachery played on her mother. She returned all the money and jewellery and put them at the feet of her mother and said, 'Amma, your blessings are worth more than lakhs of rupees. Keep these trinkets with you. God knows how much adversity you may have to face yet.'

Phulmati was about to say something when Umanath came into the room and said, 'What are you doing, Kumud? Come on, hurry up. It is getting late. The people are in a desperate hurry. Well, you will be back here in two or four months, then you can take whatever you may.'

Phulmati felt as if Umanath had rubbed salt on her injuries. Stung, she shot back, 'What is there left with me that I will give her? Go, beti, may your husband have a long life.'

Kumud went away. Phulmati, struck with grief, collapsed on the ground. The last hope she had nurtured had extinguished.

6

One year passed.

Of all the rooms in the house, Phulmati's room was the largest and well ventilated. She had vacated it for her eldest bahu for several months and was herself occupying a small room, living like a beggar. She was now without any attachment for her sons and their wives. Her position was that of a maid in the house. Nothing that passed in the house, neither any person nor any object was of any concern to her. She was living only because she had not yet died. She was unaffected by any joy or pain. Umanath opened his clinic. His friends had a grand party, with revelries and celebration. Dayanath opened his printing press. There was another party. Sitanath got a scholarship and went off to a foreign land.

There were celebrations yet again. At the *yagyopavita* ceremony of Kamatanath's eldest son, there was a big bash, but not a glimmer of happiness could be seen on Phulmati's face. Kamatanath was bedridden with typhoid for a month and hardly survived. In order to garner more publicity for his newspaper, Dayanath wrote an objectionable article for which he was sentenced to six months' imprisonment. Umanath took a bribe, filed a false report in a criminal case and his legal licence was seized, but there was not the slightest regret on Phulmati's face. It was as if there was no hope, no interest, and no worries left in her life. Her life was limited to doing just two things: she worked mechanically like a beast, and took her food. An animal may be goaded to work, but it eats of its own accord. Phulmati worked without any stimulus but ate food as if she was nibbling at some poisonous crumbs. For months she did not bother to oil her hair, or wash her clothes, and just didn't care. She was bereft of all sensations.

The Sawan rains came intermittently, spreading malaria. There were dark clouds in the sky and the earth flooded with muddy water. The humid air spread around, giving people cold, fever and asthma. The maid of the house fell sick. Phulmati, soaked to the skin in the rain, did all the work and cleaned all the pots and pans. Then she made a fire and put the pans on it. The boys must have their meals on time. Suddenly, she remembered that Kamatanath was not used to drinking tap water. She set out to fetch Gangajal though it was raining.

Kamatanath reclining on his bed saw her and said, 'Forget it, Amma, I shall go and get the water. The maid and the *Kahar* are both absent today.'

Phulmati looked at the sky darkening with clouds and said, 'Beta, you will get drenched and catch cold.'

'But you too are wet. You may fall sick.'

Phulmati said nonchalantly, 'I will not fall sick. God has made me immortal.'

Umanath was sitting close by. He was not earning much from his clinic, which constantly worried him. He looked towards his brother and the sister-in-law and remarked, 'Let her go, bhaiya. She has lorded it over her bahus for a long time, let her do some atonement.'

The Ganga was swollen like an ocean. The horizon met the farthest shore. The riverside trees had only their tops trailing on the water and the ghats were completely submerged. Phulmati came down the steps carrying her pitcher. She filled water in it and as she was climbing the steps she slipped, couldn't balance herself and fell into the water. For some time, she desperately thrashed her limbs and then she was sucked into the waves. A couple of pandas saw her and shouted, 'Look, run, the old woman is drowning. Some ran to save her but Phulmati was drowned in the whirling, threatening waves that would make anyone's heart quiver.

Someone asked, 'Who was this old woman?'

'Arré, she is Pandit Ayodhyanath's widow.'

'But Ayodhyanath was a big man.'

'Yes, indeed he was, but she was doomed to be buffeted by misfortune.'

'He has many sons who are quite well-off and have huge incomes.'

'Yes, that is true, but after all, there is something known as destiny.'

Translated from the Hindi by Satish C. Aikant

Notes

Tulia

First published as 'Devi' in *Chand* (April 1935), and later included in *Gupt Dhan* 2 (1962). In Urdu, it was compiled in *Kulliyaat-e Premchand* 14 (2003) under the title 'Wafa ki Devi'.

Sati

First published in Hindi as 'Sati' in *Chandan* (March 1927), and later included in *Mansarovar* 4 (1939). In Urdu it was published in *Aakhiri Tohfa* (1934). Now available in *Kulliyaat-e Premchand* 12 (2003).

The Goddess from Heaven

First published in Hindi as 'Swarg ki Devi' in *Chand* (November, 1925), and later included in *Mansarovar* 3 (1938). In Urdu it was included in the collection *Prem*

Chaleesi (1930) as 'Jannat ki Devi'. Now available in *Kulliyaat-e Premchand* 11 (2001).

The Accusation

First published in Hindi with the title 'Laanchan' in Madhuri (February 1931), and later collected in *Mansarovar* 5 (1946). In Urdu, it was published in *Chandan* (July 1932), and collected in *Zaad-e Raah* (1936). Now available in *Kulliyaat-e Premchand* 13 (2003).

Godavari's Suicide

First published in Hindi bearing the title 'Saut' in *Saraswati* (December 1915) and collected in *Mansarovar* 8 (1950). It was published in Urdu with the same title in *Prem Batteesi* 1 (1920). Now available in *Kulliyaat-e Premchand* 10 (2001).

The Co-wife

First published in Hindi as 'Saut' in *Vishal Bharat* (December 1931), and later collected in *Gupt Dhan* 2 (1962). Not available in Urdu. Transliterated from Hindi to Urdu for *Kulliyaat-e Premchand* 13 (2003).

Two Sisters

First published in Urdu as 'Do Bahnein' in *Asmat* (October 1935), and later included in *Doodh ki Qeemat* (1937). Now available in Urdu in *Kulliyaat-e Premchand* 14 (2003). In

Hindi, it was published in *Madhuri* (August 1936), and included in *Kafan* (1937).

A Positive Change

First published in Hindi with the title 'Vidhwans' in *Aaj* (July 1921), and later collected in *Prem Pacheesi* (1923) and *Mansarovar* 8 (1950). It was published in Urdu with the title 'Tahreek-e Khair' in *Humayun* (April 1922), and collected much later in *Kulliyaat-e Premchand* 10 (2001).

This story has two radically different endings in the two versions. This is the alternate ending in the Hindi version:

> . . . He looked towards the oven of the old woman and his entire body rankled with an anger that spread like fire. She did not even have an inkling of doubt that she was doing something against the zamindar. She could not even imagine that anger can have such an eternal life. A gifted man can have so much malice against a poor, frail woman; she had no inkling of such a thing. Given her nature, she considered human character much higher than that. But lo! Unfortunate one! You've grown grey hair without gaining any wisdom!
>
> At once Thakur shouted at her, 'Who gave you the order?'
>
> Bhungi was taken aback to see the venerable zamindar standing in front. Thakur demanded once again, 'Who gave you the permission for this?' Scared, Bhungi said, 'Everybody desired that I should rebuild it.'
>
> 'I will have it dug up again.' Having said this, he kicked the oven. The wet clay crumbled. The second

kick was aimed at the trough but the old woman came in between and it landed on her waist. Now she got angry. Patting her waist, she said,

'I serve you, where else should I look for food?' 'Only if you stay in the village can you work for me.'

'I can only perform my duties when I make the oven. Can't I do my work to stay in the village?'

'Go, leave the village.'

Bhungi stood dejected near the oven and looked at its fiery remains, reminded of the kingdom of Lanka after it was destroyed by fire.

Within moments her frail body became one with the fire. Just then the storm blew in with great ferocity. The ascending flames ran towards the east. There were many huts of the farmers near the oven; they were all devoured by the wild flames. In this way, encouraged, the flames shot up further. Nearby there was Thakur's land, it also came under its grasp. Now there was commotion in the village. Preparations were being made to put out the fire. But the splashes of water acted as fuel to the fire. The flames flared up and Panditji's great mansion also came under its claws. And, in no time, the mansion, tossing like a ship in tumultuous waves, was drowned in the huge sea of fire and the sound of lamentation that became apparent with the remnants of the ashes was more pitiful than Bhungi's mournful wailing.

Extract translated from the Hindi by M. Asaduddin

The Condemned

First published as 'Dhikkar' in *Chand* (February 1925), and later included in *Mansarovar* 1 (1936) . Not available in the Urdu version. Transliterated from Hindi to Urdu for *Kulliyaat-e Premchand* 11 (2001).

The Widow with Sons

First published as 'Betonwali Vidhva' in Hindi in *Chand* (November 1932), and later included in *Mansarovar* 7 (1947). In Urdu, it was published in the collection *Zaad-e Raah* (1936) under the title 'Badnaseeb Ma'. Now available in *Kulliyaat-e Premchand* 14 (2003).

Note on Translators

Anuradha Ghosh teaches in the Department of English at Jamia Millia Islamia, New Delhi. Her specialization is in the area of literature, cinema and culture studies. Presently, she is working on an Indian Council of Social Science Research project on the Muslim question in Bengali and Malayalam cinema.

Bharti Arora has completed her PhD from the Department of English at Jamia Millia Islamia, New Delhi. She teaches at Janki Devi Memorial College, Delhi University.

Kalyanee Rajan teaches English at Shaheed Bhagat Singh Evening College, New Delhi. Her areas of interest are Indian writing in English and translation.

Neerja M. Chand is reader of English at Ram Lal Anand College, Delhi University. She completed her MA in English from the University of Wisconsin, USA, and has a PhD in African literature

Satish C. Aikant is former professor of English at HNB Garhwal University and a former fellow of the Indian Institute of Advanced Study, Shimla. He has been a visiting professor at Ecole des Hautes Etudes en Sciences Sociales, Paris, and the editor of *Summerhill: IIAS Review*.

Shaifta Ayoub is assistant professor of English at Government Degree College, Nawa Kadal, Srinagar, Jammu and Kashmir. Her areas of interest include translation studies, comparative literature and postcolonial studies.

Shailendra Kumar Singh is pursuing his PhD from Jamia Millia Islamia, New Delhi. He has a master's in English literature from Hindu College, Delhi University. His research interests include peasant narratives, gender studies and Premchand's literary corpus.

Shirin Bismillah is an MPhil student of English at Jamia Millia Islamia, New Delhi.

Swati Pal teaches in the Department of English at Janki Devi Memorial College, Delhi University. She is currently the officiating principal of the college. Her areas of interest are modern drama, creative writing, education and translation.